PRAISE FOR *Sugaring Off*

"A beautifully human novel about secret lives and chance encounters. In *Sugaring Off*, Fanny Britt writes with wisdom, tenderness, and razor sharpness about those moments of collision that remake a life. She dares to surface the lines of accident and fate that pulse between us—when it is a stranger and not an intimate who leads us back to ourselves. A novel operatic and cosmic in scale, but delivered with a visceral swiftness and sensitivity, *Sugaring Off* is gorgeous, profound, and never without humour."
—Claudia Dey, author of *Daughter*

"*Sugaring Off* is a stunning exploration of class and privilege, and our desperate need for connection. In this deftly written story, Fanny Britt explores the dissolution of relationships, regret and grief, and how we navigate the consequences of our actions. A truly exceptional novel."
—Lindsay Zier-Vogel, author of *Letters to Amelia*

"An accurate, uncomplacent depiction of Western society and of the disparity that exists between classes and ethnicities, this brilliantly written story joins the family of great North American novels and asks one fundamental question: however privileged we may be, is it possible to live without relying on others? In this clever and lucid fresco, complex characters are confronted with crises which are not unconnected to the paradoxes inhabiting them."
—Governor General's Literary Award
for French-Language Fiction Jury Citation

# FANNY BRITT

## SUGARING OFF

TRANSLATED BY SUSAN OURIOU

LITERATURE IN TRANSLATION SERIES

BOOK*HUG PRESS
TORONTO 2024

FIRST ENGLISH EDITION

First published as *Faire les sucres* by Fanny Britt © 2021 by Le Cheval d'août éditeur.
Published through the intermediary of the literary agent Milena Ascione—BOOKSAGENT—
France (booksagent.fr).
English Translation © 2024 by Susan Ouriou

*Library and Archives Canada Cataloguing in Publication*

Title: Sugaring off / Fanny Britt ; translated by Susan Ouriou.
Other titles: Faire les sucres. English
Names: Britt, Fanny, author.
Series: Literature in translation series.
Description: First English edition. | Series statement: Literature in translation series |
    Translation of: Faire les sucres. | In English, translated from the French.
Identifiers: Canadiana (print) 20240345657 | Canadiana (ebook) 20240345665
    ISBN 9781771669085 (softcover) | ISBN 9781771669115 (EPUB)
Subjects: LCGFT: Novels.
Classification: LCC PS8603.R5877 F3513 2024 | DDC C843/.6—dc23

The production of this book was made possible through the generous assistance of the Canada
Council for the Arts and the Ontario Arts Council. Book*hug Press also acknowledges the
support of the Government of Canada through the Canada Book Fund and the Government
of Ontario through the Ontario Book Publishing Tax Credit and the Ontario Book Fund.

Book*hug Press acknowledges that the land on which it operates is the traditional territory
of many nations, including the Mississaugas of the Credit, the Anishnabeg, the Chippewa,
the Haudenosaunee, and the Wendat peoples. We also recognize the enduring presence of
many diverse First Nations, Inuit, and Métis peoples and are grateful for the opportunity
to meet and work on this territory.

I'm happy with myself the way I am,
more desiring than desirable.
—Virginie Despentes, *King Kong Theory*

You have everything, and so much of it.
—Peggy to Don, *Mad Men*

# CONTENTS

2002

1

The Beach

9

2008

129

The Sugaring Off

137

Celia

197

2002

HE'D SIT HER DOWN ON A STOOL BY THE FAN AND SHE'D watch him at work. First, he poured the sugar into the large copper pot, and Celia imagined it turning into a band's kettle drum after dark. Sometimes, to amuse her, he'd unhook one of the big wooden spoons hanging from the wall and drum with all his might on the pot's rounded surface, giving off a deep, vibrant timbre that captivated Celia. So she'd clap and say, "More! More!" and her grandfather would comply. Jeffrey and his friends' shouts of glee echoed outside. Celia could never understand why her brother preferred playing under the marina's pilotis instead of staying inside for the show. What could be better?

After the sugar came time for the corn syrup, concentrated milk, and vanilla. As it boiled, the mixture gave off a sweet fragrance, diluted at first, then increasingly strong, almost acrid.

"Smell that, Celia? You've got to keep careful tabs on that smell," he warned her. "It tells you when it's almost ready. When the smell is too faint, that means you have to wait. Too strong, and it's burnt. You must be sure to catch it at the right time and not let any of it get away."

Celia nodded and glanced over at her mother, who was busy arranging large metal rods in the shape of a rectangle to contain the taffy on the cooling table.

"The same as for a man," her mother said with dry humour.

Her grandfather shook his head but laughed all the same. Celia knew he was her mother's father but didn't understand what that really meant. How could you be a grandfather and a father at the same time? If Granddad Herb was her mother's father, then what was Julian, her own father, to her mother? He wasn't her sweetheart the way Grandma Clara had been her granddad's sweetheart. Come to think of it, he wasn't really a dad either, not like the other kids had, who carried the coolers for their picnics and fixed their cars on Saturdays, lying on their backs on the pavement. Julian lived on the other side of the world, on boats that fished out people who'd been thrown into the sea with their belongings. Sometimes he came to visit them, slept on the couch, drank coffee all morning, put songs on the record player, and closed his eyes, saying, "Did I ever miss this." Then he'd be off again and send postcards that her mother read out loud to them. Jeffrey kept them all in a shoebox.

Whenever her mother took her to the Oak Bluffs arcade, Celia was quick to bypass the merry-go-round and the fortune-telling machines—she hated the empty eyes in those mechanical faces and the card they spat out that was supposed to reveal some secret about her. She always took a detour so as not to have to see them. Instead she watched the big ships coming and going, their bellies full of cars and vacationers. Although she didn't actually expect to see Julian in the crowd, something

4

kept bringing her back to the water's edge. "How come I always only see the water rising and never falling?" she sometimes asked. Her mother would say, "It's just a coincidence. One day you'll see the ebbing tide." But Celia gave her head a stubborn shake. *You don't understand.*

Once the batch was ready, her grandfather and her mother each grabbed a handle and carried the pot together, their steps perfectly synchronized, over to the cooling table where they poured out the boiled sugar. Celia watched as the liquid, sometimes white, sometimes golden, fanned across the large marble table till the metal rods stopped its advance. It was like the surface of a lake, almost a mirror. Celia imagined that if you were to dive inside, you'd find yourself in Candy Land, where chewing gum grows on trees and flowers are made of licorice, just like in the game she saw at Heather's house at the birthday party she'd been invited to. She loved the pictures so much she'd wanted to eat the board they were printed on.

Before the mixture hardened, her mother sprinkled coarse grains of sea salt overtop, then folded it in two, in four, then in eight, like a blanket. Next she slid her forearms underneath and carried it—it looked so heavy!—over to the puller, whose arms began to shake with a tired rattling sound.

"It's getting noisier and noisier," said Celia's mother.

"It's been working since 1934," her father replied. "Mark my words, you'll be making at least as much noise when you're that old."

They laughed again.

Stretched taut, the taffy shone as though tiny gold threads lay hidden inside the liquid.

Celia's mother added a flavour or colour from the dozens of bottles stored on the shelves in the back of the shop, then rolled the paste ever longer and thinner into the shape of an unending sugar snake. Soon they'd buy an extruder; it was too hard on the shoulders and arms to keep doing it by hand. "I'm okay spending my life in this cramped kitchen sweating over a boiling pot," her mother said, "but I have no desire to end up looking like Mr. T." Celia didn't know who Mr. T was, she imagined a blue figure in the shape of a T, like the characters in the Mr. Men/Little Miss books: *Mr. Musclebound*.

The double-twist candy-wrapping machine was Celia's favourite. The snake was slowly swallowed up by two bright red metal spools that cut it into small cubes and wrapped them in wax paper bearing the logo of her grandparents' store. She knew the shop's name came from her grandmother. Clara's Saltwater Taffy. Her picture hung above the front door. She's shown standing in front of the store window. She's laughing, her thick-framed glasses masking her eyes, and wiping one hand on her white apron, the other resting on the head of a little girl about Celia's age, four or five at the most, clinging to her leg. Her mother, Rhonda. In the background, leaning against the door frame, stands Herbert, a cigarette drooping from his mouth. Celia hadn't seen her grandfather smoke ever since the doctor warned him he wouldn't live past his sixties if he kept it up, and did he want to die like his wife before he reached retirement age?

Celia didn't know what retirement was, but she knew she wished Clara had reached that age. Whenever Rhonda spoke of her, there was a lilt to her voice.

Granddad Herb let Celia help him during the last stage, packing the taffy into white cardboard boxes fitted with a small cellophane window to give a glimpse of what was inside. An equal number of mint, vanilla, cherry, caramel, chocolate, and lemon taffies had to be placed inside each one. Once the box was full, it was time to close the lid that still sported her grandmother's name. Every Saturday and Sunday, they'd sell out of their entire stock before closing time. At the height of summer, they'd sell out even on weekdays.

Celia said, "Everyone has heard of Clara's taffies."

And Herb responded, "Of course, they're the best."

Celia curled up on the bench in the window and waited for the next visitors to discover, wonderstruck, the existence of their kingdom.

# The Beach

# 1

THE DAY HE JUST ABOUT DIED, ADAM DUMONT SPOTTED an American TV star in Chilmark's general store on the island of Martha's Vineyard, the vacation spot chosen that summer for Marion, him, and another couple. Much later, when the chance sighting had taken on the allure of an anecdote, this is how he would tell it: The day I just about died, I saw the actor from *The Office*, uh-huh, the one married to that beautiful English actress, no, she wasn't there, yes, it was earlier that same day, before the accident, no, he looked preoccupied, we didn't want to bother him. The incident had an ironic twist difficult to put one's finger on. Was it really ironic to bump into a well-known public figure who, incidentally, meant nothing to you, on the day death nearly spirited you away? Was it ironic because the day seemed to hold such promise, one of those days that yields a good yarn on your return from holidays, *wait till you hear, you'll never guess who we saw in Chilmark's general store*, was it ironic that a day that paid off so well in celebrity sightings— an actual sport in Martha's Vineyard, like the sightings of birds, whales, caribou elsewhere—should end in a near-drowning in the Atlantic Ocean? Most likely *ironic* wasn't the best term to describe the juxtaposition of the two events. *Ironic* was, perhaps, even a bit indecent. Adam wouldn't know for sure till much later. For the longest time, he wouldn't know much of anything, and the troubling sorrow that weighed on him from July 19, 2017 onward would at times prevent him from forming complete sentences or finding the right words, or *saying* anything at all. So *ironic* was probably not the right word, but it was the only one he could come up with to speak of it.

Marion had suggested they rent a house on Martha's Vineyard because its local food movement was flourishing, and Adam, keenly interested in the trend, would be able to mix business with pleasure, and she knew how tough it was for him to leave all work behind—she wasn't wrong, it was even a source of pride for him, he loved being a so-called workaholic. Down there, she said, people didn't worry about paying more for quality food, and Adam would enjoy seeing it for himself. They would visit farms open to the public whose owners had no hesitation about sharing the results of their farming methods so the greatest number could benefit. She'd learned that somewhere, in a magazine or the travel section of the *New York Times*, which she read every Sunday despite the over six hundred kilometres separating New York from their house in Hudson, northwest of Montreal. "We'll pretend we live in Hudson, New York," she'd said two years earlier when they'd signed the commitment to purchase the lot on which they would build the house of their dreams. Marion quite liked the United States and found it almost cruel that Quebec was so close to the mythical places that inspired her—Cape Cod, Chicago, Nashville—yet too far to actually live there, all the while recognizing that the Canadian border protected them from the absurdities of life in the States—guns and arrogance, injustice and materialism—all of which scandalized her. But, in all honesty, who didn't prefer the sandy beaches of Cape Cod, the bona fide waters of the Atlantic, the lobster shacks and the cobblestone streets found along the eastern American coast to the pebbles of the beaches on the Gaspé Peninsula, the blackflies, the villages that cared nothing for beauty?

"How dare you judge me?" she asked when Adam teased her about her contradictions. The question was a rhetorical one. Adam was just as seduced by the region and by Americans' entrepreneurial spirit as by their admitted fondness for material comforts. It wouldn't have crossed his mind to judge Marion for something so trivial; it would have meant judging himself, which was not Adam's thing.

Shortly afterward, Marion suggested they invite Julie and Simon along, which Adam declared to be a good idea and he meant it. They often spent holidays together. Like him, Simon liked to stay up late, and together they drank rare, notable spirits. Whenever he thought back on those days, he always felt like they'd been extremely close, even though, in actual fact, neither of them opened up much about their feelings. Problems at work, aging parents, nostalgia for their teen years in the eighties—was there anything else? Simon talked about the daughter he and Julie had had later in life, and worshipped everything she did. Adam played along, sharing his memories of the childhoods of his children, Félix and Adèle, newly minted adults whom he hadn't seen on a daily basis for quite some time now. Marion had suggested inviting them, too, and

Adam wondered whether it was out of a sense of duty or to please him or in response to the maternal instinct she had to direct somewhere, given she had no child of her own. Not that it mattered; neither of them would have come.

Their mother had refrained from leading an active smear campaign against him, as far as he knew in any case. The children had never openly showed any hostility toward Marion either. Perhaps it was worse, though, perhaps they were simply indifferent to the life Adam led, Marion thought in moments of angst. After all, she was thirty-nine. Adam, who was eight years older, hadn't had what was referred to as a mid-life crisis, for lack of a better term to describe the intense turmoil that strikes out of the blue, felling you midstream, keeping you awake at night, eyes wide open, heart racing at the thought of the inescapable future and, worse yet, the irrecoverable past. At forty, Adam was the host of a TV show, which—on the strength of his title as a "chef in vogue"—bore his name. His restaurant, DNA, was a great success, attracting hockey players, movie directors, young politicians, and "visionary" architects— or at least that's what the newspapers wrote. His partner had convinced him to open up a second, then a third, restaurant. Ever since his business had grown, Adam found himself spending less time out with the guests or in the kitchen and more time in meetings. *Adam à table*, an immediate hit on TV, had allowed him to leave the kitchen behind, a fact he only bemoaned for appearances' sake. In truth, the constraints of his profession had begun to weigh on him and he liked having evenings free to see friends, eat in others' restaurants, and attend the premières and shows he was invited to. He saw his children every other weekend, a schedule that suited him just fine, although he didn't boast about it. His other friends who were divorced had taken on joint custody, or that's what the fathers thought, Marion pointed out, since a day less here or there added up to whole weeks and months by the time the end of the year rolled round. But that was the point: Adam's friends didn't count the days, and most had started a new life with another woman, often having one or more babies, babies they looked after with her, which served as an excuse for all kinds of things, don't you think, don't we all have certain limits? The same men who had trouble acknowledging there might be any issues had no trouble drawing boundaries when the time came to ask for adjustments to the custody arrangement, at least not according to Marion's girlfriends.

Adam didn't feel that those grievances applied to him. Sarah, the mother of his children, had never asked him for joint custody. Time and again, she had said that Félix and Adèle were her whole life and that having to grieve a united family had been bad enough, could he please not add to the weight she was already carrying by tearing her little ones away from her one week out of every two? Plus, their father spent his evenings at the restaurant, so what would he arrange for them on weeknights? Would they have to do their homework somewhere between the sauce prep area and the bread oven? Had he forgotten that Adèle was susceptible to migraines and needed a regular schedule and a stable environment, and that Félix had to be at the arena three times a week for hockey practice; the arena was so close to her house, it wasn't Sarah's fault that Adam went and bought himself a condo in Mile

End when the children had only ever lived in Rosemont. Over time, and after his move to Hudson, the children, now grown, let more time elapse between their visits, and then Félix moved out on his own. It was all an easy transition.

Adam didn't want to hurt anyone, and he loved them—Sarah, Félix, Adèle—and didn't want them to suffer. Deep down he was convinced they would suffer more from a disruption to their routine than from their father's absence, and he felt almost magnanimous letting Sarah make the decisions for the family.

"See how I acknowledge your expertise," he'd have said had he been able to formulate the thought.

And Sarah would have answered, "I see that you acknowledge my expertise, it was the best gift you could have given me, time with my children, thank you, Adam."

He was proud of his arrangement with her and often said that he and Sarah had had a successful divorce.

THE DAY HE JUST ABOUT DIED, ADAM DUMONT DID NOT have sex. Usually, holidays fostered intimacy. They drank every evening, and alcohol made Marion languorous. Adam adored the fragrance of her skin in summer, the scent of a recently downed Aperol spritz, and she let the bedside lamp shine on her hips and ankles and breasts and climbed onto him like a beautifully framed movie star. On vacation, they usually made love every night and sometimes on waking as well. Not that he kept count. But this time, the layout of the rooms in the house they'd rented was less than ideal. The wall to their room gave onto their friends' bedroom and, the day before, Julie had confided in Marion that their love life was non-existent: the most they could manage was a periodic coming together in the hope of conceiving one last baby, but she was at the point where she dreaded that quick, fumbling contact, that adolescent embrace that had nothing to do with their first years together, and actually, if Simon was cheating on her, it wouldn't be all that bad, guilt weighed more heavily on her than jealousy, she'd said, and Marion detected a note of sadness in her voice and so had trouble taking her at her word. Out of consideration for Julie—for Julie and Simon—she would rather not torment them with their own creaking mattress and moans of uninhibited lovemaking. Adam thought it very thoughtful of her, which turned him on.

He didn't talk about that sort of thing with either Simon or his other male friends. Contrary to what people might think, Adam had had very little exposure to locker-room talk. He did play sports and the guys he played with had, how to put it, done their fair share of living. They did occasionally mention, under their breath, since they didn't like the sour facial expressions that came along with it, marital or extramarital gossip about couples in their circle. But Adam never confessed to his friends how Marion's moral rectitude turned him on. She had been known to give him an erection just by revealing she'd refused to bill a patient for a root canal because the patient's mother had broken her hip and would have to be moved to assisted living, which would cost a fortune that the patient, a single mother, did not have. Marion simply jotted down *one filling* on the file, the patient ended up paying no more than a hundred dollars or so, and afterward Marion was treated to Adam's generosity. Over the years, Marion had cottoned on to Adam's weakness for her empathetic traits, and it tickled her. Adam wondered whether she didn't sometimes exaggerate the extent of her caring gestures in order to obtain his favours—a hypothesis that was not without pleasing him—but that night, in the bedroom with mint-coloured walls in the house on Boston Hill Road, Marion insisted they respect her desire for discretion. She promised that when Julie and Simon took Philomène on a bike ride the next afternoon, she would be all his and he all hers.

AS IT TURNED OUT, THAT NEXT AFTERNOON, ADAM SAT waiting his turn in the emergency room of the Oak Bluffs hospital and they only made love nine days later, back in Quebec. Right after the orgasm, he felt pain. Akin to pressure in his thorax. An ache in his chest? Did he still have water in his lungs? Was it possible he was a victim of secondary drowning? He'd looked it up on his computer, in both French and English—*Temps maximal pour noyade secondaire. Maximal delay time for secondary drowning.* Often, English gave more results. Marion could tell his mind was elsewhere, but she said nothing—there are worse things during lovemaking. Once again, her thoughtfulness touched then excited Adam, and with increasing ardour, he grasped her hips with something like despair, then let himself fall almost roughly on her—almost since Adam didn't like the idea of hurting Marion, that sort of thing didn't turn him on—and when Marion turned to him, her face was awash in tears.

"Because I almost lost you," she said when he asked why she was crying. "I just about lost you and I didn't lose you."

It took Adam Dumont ages to fall asleep that night, as on the previous nights, as on the nights to follow.

Each time he managed to close his eyes after an hour or two spent watching one episode after another of some mindless cop series, his laptop propped up on a pillow in front of him, the accident would play again in his head and wake him with a start. A jolt he received as a reproach: *How can you sleep when that poor girl is suffering? How can you sleep when you just about died?* He understood then that he would keep reliving scenes from the collision, the rough contact with the board, the wave that swept him under, the sand that slid beneath the lining of his bathing suit, the undertow tugging at his body, neither ocean bed nor surface for endless seconds, the water he'd swallowed feeling more like a litre than a mouthful; then, once he emerged, his burning throat still raked by salt the next day, the girl's face, the girl's blood, the girl's knee that refused to bend the right way, the only logically possible way, the initial disgust he felt at the sight of her dislocated knee quickly followed by shame, after all, he was the one responsible for that shattered knee, had he not been the one to bear down on her? Well, she could have chosen not to lead the little boy so close to the surfers; she could have paid attention. But wasn't she entitled like everyone else to enjoy the beach without wondering if some thrill-seeking idiot would have so little control over his board that he'd make a beeline for the little boy she would have to scoop up in extremis because that was the way of it, children first, and, in rescuing him, she herself had sunk into the thick sand the wave had whipped up and so couldn't avoid some idiot's surfboard as it crashed into her knee and threw her onto the shore, the child still held out at arm's length, blinded by July's bright sun?

Yet Adam had done everything possible to avoid hitting her. He had leaned way back, just as Simon had shown him, his weight on his heels, pretending he was on a skateboard in the waves, Simon had laughed, not that you're a pro in that arena either! Adam's and Simon's teasing of one another masked love, and love masked rivalry, and Adam saw it as a healthy progression. For him, friendship was both a pressure valve and a springboard, but he couldn't stand sentimentality; he would never have been able to tell his friend that he loved him, those words only left his mouth with a woman or at a child's bedside, and even then, the child couldn't be too old. Somewhere between eight and ten the curtain of propriety dropped and, although he never stopped loving his children, he quit telling them so—in birthday cards, yes, in the flourish of giving at Christmas and graduation, too, maybe once or twice in an awkward text message, which, he'd noticed, quickly dampened the mood—so with them, he usually stuck to little yellow faces or sometimes a cat's head with eyes in the shape of a heart. With Simon, they had a complex series of inside jokes and sardonic comments about mutual friends that served as their glue, which he liked, he'd sometimes reread their text messages and feel his heart swell: how lucky to have friends, what great, good fortune.

He'd leaned back, but the board failed to execute the expected turn. He felt he should straighten up to avoid losing his balance and falling into the water (why had it been so important to keep his balance, he now wondered, what did balance have to offer other than postponing the collision?), so he did, and that's when his left foot slipped, and his whole body dropped onto his surfboard, accelerating its forward motion toward the girl whose silhouette was all he could see now, a black bathing suit with two long stripes, one yellow, one pink. A disco suit, like the ones his girl cousins used to wear in the sixties. She wore shorts, too, faded red terry-cloth shorts that clashed with the suit. When he fell, he scraped his thigh on the board and it hurt, so he cried out, and just then the wave swallowed him whole, and that's when he just about died. The day he just about died, Adam Dumont did not die, but he did shatter the knee of a nineteen-year-old girl, a stranger, whose name was Celia Smith and who had one hazel eye and one eye flecked with grey, like a storm at sea in an acrylic painting. Marion would tell him later that that trait had a name, heterochromia. Adam would forget the word, but the look in Celia Smith's eyes—never.

## 2

MARION ROBERT HAD NOT ALWAYS WANTED TO BE A DENTIST. As a little girl, her thoughts hadn't turned to possible future professions, but instead to the peppers in the garden, the rhubarb under the veranda, the beehives in the field. To the whir of the sewing machine, baseball games on TV, holidays in Nova Scotia. To whether Fabiola was her friend, or whether Rachel was not anymore. To the sensual delight she came upon by chance when rubbing a spaniel-shaped stuffie between her legs under her snowman-patterned sheet. Of which she would never speak, yet would still grant herself that pleasure even as an adult, almost daily. *What do you want to be when you grow up, Marion?* The question paralyzed her, the way you stop dead when a stranger accosts you in a foreign language. Not only did she not recognize the meaning of the question, she also couldn't figure out what the expected answer would be. Should you be sincere and confess that you don't have the faintest idea and, if possible, you wouldn't work at all but would live in a castle like the Lavigueurs, who had only to buy a lottery ticket to become millionaires? Or should you be adorable, make an impression, say something cute and satisfying, *I want to be a vet because I love animals*, which was neither true nor false, neither a lie nor a plan; yes, Marion supposed she should answer, *I want to be a vet*, so that's what she did for the longest time and everyone was happy.

Then one day, an elderly second cousin said, "You could be a dentist like your dad!" And around the table, there was a rumble of approval, and her father laughed, eyes lowered, and Marion sensed something in that bowed head, those eyes staring at the tablecloth, those fingers clutching a paper napkin. Her father was touched to think his daughter might follow in his footsteps, might admire him enough to choose the same profession as him, even taking over his clinic or, why not, becoming his partner; he wouldn't be retiring any day soon, after all; ROBERT AND DAUGHTER, DENTISTS, it could say or, no, she was entitled to her name there as well, ROBERT AND ROBERT, DENTISTS, now that sounded better. So Marion, who loved nothing more than knowing that others loved her, said, "You're right, what a great idea."

It worked out. Enrolled in health sciences in a private college on the west side of Montreal, she soon saw that, among her cohort, only future dentists interested her. The students going into research were cerebral and spent Friday evenings playing obscure medieval games, while the aspiring doctors reeked of self-confidence. On the other hand, she found the future dentists to be down-to-earth, sociable, the unpretentious, happy-go-lucky sort who wanted nothing more than the good life. The different milieus the students had grown up in might have partly explained that observation; however, at seventeen, you forget to give things due consideration, to take a look at the students at the back of the class who, neither cerebral nor self-important, would also become doctors, researchers, dentists, or those who, once in university, would switch tracks and become sculptors and guidance counsellors, or others still who would drop out, commit suicide, catch malaria in Togo during a humanitarian mission, return to their native Saguenay, and, plagued by debilitating social phobia, resort to temp jobs to make ends meet.

When she thought back on her studies, Marion could, at times, have regrets.

JUST BEFORE THEIR TRIP TO MARTHA'S VINEYARD, A FORMER classmate of Marion's showed up in the clinic where she worked, in the same offices where her father had spent the last decade of his career. Her parents had decided to sell the family home in Oka and move to the city and a new condo complex that came with an elevator so Gisèle and her arthritis-afflicted feet would no longer suffer on the stairs of their hundred-year-old home. Raymond had hesitated about closing his practice. On the internet, the daily commute looked to be forty minutes there and back. In reality, the trip could take up to an hour and a quarter, and Gisèle said, "Raymond, don't even think it, it's too far. Let's keep the house instead. I've put up with the pain this long, there's no reason why I can't continue."

Raymond and Gisèle loved one another with a passionate, guilty love, each convinced that they represented a source of constant stress for the other, when the opposite was true. Raymond would have done anything for Gisèle, and Gisèle for Raymond, and for that reason, selling the house, then closing down the Oka clinic, had been a tough decision. Without

Myriam's—Marion's older sister and the cool-headed one in the family—ironic outburst in exasperation, "Wait till you're dead, then, that way you won't have to make a decision," they might still have been floundering around in a puddle of ambivalence. Eventually, the couple left behind both house and job to move to the island of Montreal, and Raymond accepted the offer from a younger colleague whose office in Pierrefonds had a vacant room just a stone's throw from their condo in old Pointe-Claire.

Still a student at the time, Marion never thought that the clinic would become her domain. She hadn't thought about ROBERT AND ROBERT for a long time. But a year later, as the family sat around a table in a Syrian restaurant on Avenue du Parc after Marion's graduation from the Université de Montréal's Faculty of Dentistry, Raymond announced there was an opening in their offices and, if she so desired, she could work at his side for a few years. "Five years max before I retire," he'd said, "I'm no martyr." Everyone had laughed, except Myriam, who glared at Marion, as though to say, *Over your dead body*, while Marion said, "Okay, yes, I'll think about it," suddenly realizing that, unlike her, her father had not forgotten about ROBERT AND ROBERT. Myriam choked on her wine, and Gisèle sighed, "Yes, we all know where you stand," then Myriam planted a loud kiss on her mother's cheek, saying, "You adore me," which Gisèle didn't deny. The equilibrium in their family came from the certainty that Marion was nothing like Myriam, a lawyer based in Vancouver who came to visit once a year and would never have connected the slightest feeling of joy to the thought of working day in and day out with her father. No one doubted that Myriam loved them. Simply put, she was hard-hearted.

"A fox in a family of hens," Gisèle said. "Who knows where we dug that one up. We love her, mind you. We adore her. But who knows where we unearthed her."

And Myriam shrugged and jostled Marion.

Marion saw this first job as a temporary foray into suburban life. Her years of university in Montreal had been a succession of long, narrow apartments whose woodwork had been repainted twenty times over, peopled with laughing roommates, balcony parties that went on into November—and even then, she spent many a winter evening bundled up in a coarse woollen blanket, both feet up on the wrought-iron railing, her hands wrapped round a cup of tea topped up with whisky, talking to Yara. A toque on her head, snowflakes on her shoulders. Sometimes on into the end of the semester, just before Christmas. Yara would address the cold head-on, an enemy to be overthrown. "I won't back down, you big lout!" she'd cry into the night. Marion loved that period of her life living in Côte-des-Neiges, the long walks home after evenings spent in the apartments of friends who lived farther from the university, in the Plateau, in Villeray, in Park Extension, and, back then, the city seemed so benevolent that she vowed never to leave. Except to go to New York, of course. London, maybe. San Francisco, too. But the suburbs? That would never happen. Then came her father's offer, the emotion in his eyes, and Marion's irrepressible desire to make him happy. She'd buy herself a new car. Surely she'd find a place to park along Outremont's quiet streets, not far from her apartment, the first one she'd rented on her own, a two-bedroom she'd fallen in love with on that very first visit, with its lilac bush in front of the window and its enamelled cast-iron sink. She'd listen to audiobooks on her drive to Pierrefonds, arrange her schedule to commute outside rush hour. She had to work, after all, and Marion had no desire to start up her own office.

"I can assure you, this first position will be perfectly suitable," she said over the phone to Myriam, who retorted, "With each passing day, your vocabulary brings me one step closer to turning to antidepressants."

It was a surprise for Marion to find herself still there twelve years later, but that's the way things played out. Her clientele was pleasant, and she had to admit she had enjoyed the ten years spent at her father's side.

"You said five years, Raymond," Gisèle hinted gently six, then seven, then eight years after Marion started at the clinic.

It wasn't exactly a reproach. But all the same, their daughter, so generous, so devoted to others, shouldn't be stifled.

Gisèle had no favourites, children were a gift from life, but it had to be said: Marion was an exemplary daughter. The label galled that same daughter, although she wasn't sure exactly why. Had she not earned it? So, invariably, she said that her father could stay as long as he liked.

In the end, the lure of gardening in the summer and travelling to other cultures in the winter won him over, and Raymond retired with the half-heavy, half-thrilled heart of those heading for the horizon as seen from the edge of a cliff. He offered his shares to Marion, who accepted them.

Claude, the partner in the Pierrefonds clinic, was a happy man in his fifties who had a new wife twenty years his junior with whom he went skydiving, a man who meant to live life to the fullest before he ran into erectile issues. (The very idea caused him angst since he loved having sex with Audrey, who complimented him daily on his eternal youth, praise that gave him such a thrill it almost hurt.) Did Marion ever pine for the small office she'd dreamed of for so long, an office attached to a brick house in Outremont, where she'd make her children pancakes before crossing the yard to look after the needs of the peaceful community in her neighbourhood where heritage and beauty reigned? At the time, no. By then, she was living with Adam in an impeccably renovated apartment in Mile End, and they had plans to build a modernist, glass-fronted house on nothing less than a one-acre lot—that was Adam's dream. And how could she leave her patients? She had treated pregnant women whose soon-to-be-teenaged children now came to see her. The bonds were real. Not to mention that she didn't have any children to make breakfast for before crossing that yard. Félix and Adèle buttered their own toast.

"HAVE YOU JUST MOVED INTO THE NEIGHBOURHOOD?" Marion asked the man as she tried to remember his first name. An embarrassing fact, given that she'd spent so much time sitting next to him in class. She hated seeing anyone experience the embarrassment of being forgettable, as much as she hated it when it happened to her, in other words, any time she attended a restaurant-related event—or, worse yet, a television-related one—with Adam. *Sorry, what was your name again?* And then she'd have to go back to square one, explaining who she was, how long she'd been Adam's partner, *No, not in the restaurant business, I'm a dentist, well, I don't know if it's surprising, we do need them, is your restaurant/show/supermarket partnership still doing well?* Generally speaking, one question was enough to get them started, and Marion was left with the strong conviction that they all saw her as being of no consequence. She had no desire to subject this man to the faraway look—Vincent? Julien? there was an *e*, an *i*, and an *n* in his name—to the same humiliation. Could he tell she didn't remember his name? Was he avoiding looking at her?

"I've been here a few years, actually; this is where I grew up," he replied.

"Oh, did you come back to look after your parents?"

*Hugo? Martin?* He gave a little smothered laugh, more like the sob you feel coming on watching a sad movie on the plane when you don't want to draw attention to yourself, and said, "It's kind of the opposite, I had a bout of depression and lost my job, so I'm back living with them."

Colin!

Given that he'd just revealed something distressing, Marion fought not to let her relief show at remembering his name and instead grimaced the way you do at the smell of hair dye.

"Oh, Colin, I'm sorry to hear that, was this recently?"

He said he'd been experiencing bouts of depression for quite some time now, which, in fact, was why he'd left university before finishing. His words hit Marion hard; she had no recollection of him leaving, nor of any conversation with her friends during which anyone wondered about his absence. How could he not have been depressed? No one even saw him.

Marion choked back the lump of remorse forming in her throat and stammered, "I-I had no idea, I'm so sorry. If I'd known—"

Colin shook his head as he ran a hand through his hair. "Oh, no, don't worry, I was good at hiding it. You know, you once told me that whenever you felt sad, you'd put on headphones and listen to the radio jacked all the way up and that the big hits by Haddaway and Ace of Base, as absurd and ridiculous as they were, never failed to make you laugh and, even more absurd, dance; that's what helped you feel better. I never forgot it and still turn the radio up in the car. If you ask me, though, today's hits don't work as well."

Marion felt unsettled to learn she'd made such an impression and ashamed she hadn't kept a spot for him in her own memory. Jessie came up to tell her a patient was waiting in room two and Marion had to end the conversation. "So nice of you to drop by," she said warily.

"Actually, I'm here to start a file. Personal hygiene is crucial to healing; it shows you care about yourself. According to my shrink, anyway."

Then he gave another little laugh. The same sobbing laugh that Marion kept hearing in her head as she went to bed that night, which led her to tell Adam the whole story, the sadness, the shame, the compassion, her impulse to offer Colin his first cleaning free of charge. After hearing her out, Adam rolled her onto her back, grabbed her by the waist, and pulled till her pelvis lay halfway down the bed, then buried his head between her legs.

# 3

BACK FROM THEIR HOLIDAY, AS HE OPENED THE KITCHEN'S glassed-in door that looked onto the birch trees and the neighbour's pastures below, Adam was surprised to see that the high-voltage wire was still there. As though the abomination that disfigured the landscape, framed as it was by the door's matte aluminum casing, could disappear on its own, a metaphysical symbol of the universe apologizing to him for what he'd just been through on Martha's Vineyard.

While the lot was being cleared, they'd noticed that the road behind their place was dotted with utility poles; on most of the province's roadways, wires bordered the route above the houses. What they hadn't expected, once the trees had been uprooted, the ground backfilled and the foundations poured on the highest plateau on their property, was that the wires would be visible from their window, the horizon displaced, a taut cheese-cutter wire poised to cut the space in two. Adam hated that wire with a fervour that made his friends laugh and left him suffering from prolonged fits of rage during which he went so far as to tell Marion they had to sell.

"We chose this lot for the view; if we accept that disfigurement, it's a betrayal of the whole purpose of our plan," he retorted when Marion pointed out that, by talking about it so much, he was the one spoiling the view for everyone else.

Marion indicated that no one had even noticed the wire till he brought it up and, every time, Adam felt a fleeting doubt: Was Marion an idiot? How could she not see? Marion then proceeded to ask one of her favourite questions. *What can we do?* It was not just some abstract question—she meant it.

*What can we do for the environment?* And she bought an electric car.

*What can we do for Adèle's migraines?* And she booked her an appointment with the wonderful osteopath who had rid her mother of her inner ear infection.

*What can we do to help motivate you again, sweetheart?* And she'd planned their vacation to Martha's Vineyard so Adam could gorge himself on local products. For Thanksgiving, since he'd seemed down in the dumps since their return, they'd travel to New York and scope out the organic wines being served in its new restaurants. Adam agreed to it all—he had never liked defeatists and appreciated Marion's entrepreneurial spirit. Sarah could be so taciturn, ruled by moods as exaggerated as they were incoherent, and Adam wanted nothing more than to cling to the penchant for joy that characterized their life together. And yet, that wire was the death of him, would be the death of him, was his thought on their return from Martha's Vineyard when Marion opened the curtain on the kitchen door to let in the afternoon sun. It had even seemed to him that the wire had a slight curve to it now, perhaps a bit of a droop. A curve that, to Adam, looked, for all intents and purposes, like a derisive grin.

He'd just about died yet he just about hadn't gone surfing that day. The two thoughts played constantly in his mind, as though the first depended on the second, or vice versa, he didn't know anymore. Was it that Simon had insisted on getting them moving, *Old man, let's prove to ourselves we're still alive,* just because he was, in some way, in need of a brush with death? Was there some plan at work, an inescapable chain of events? Or, on the contrary, should he have turned down the invitation, or reminded Simon that if others had let their dreams and their hard-ons die, Adam had no need to stoke his own fires, he was as solid and vibrant as he'd been on the dance floor at the unending parties they'd organized in their twenties, pulsating to the rhythm of the hypnotic techno music's bass notes; he cultivated desire and consistently achieved his goals and, no, really, he wasn't looking for any extra stimulation on his holiday, thank you very much!

Except that he'd said yes, and Simon seemed so happy at the prospect of horsing around in the water together and Julie so relieved, as though the worth of her man depended on his ability to introduce his most accomplished, most competent friend to something he himself could do better. Later, Adam remembered thinking at the time that Simon and Julie might finally make love that night and that it would be in part thanks to him.

"It'll take our mind off things," Marion had added as she gently removed a bit of sand from Philomène's hair. "Go on."

Earlier, in fact, the little one had been targeted by a fierce gull trying to rip off her beach hat with its beak, likely mistaking it for a stray cookie package or a shell shining in the sun. No matter, the creature had given everyone an awful scare, starting with Julie, who'd jumped to her feet screaming at the bird to get the hell out, shoo, go away, to the stunned gaze of her daughter, who burst into noisy sobs. Julie apologized afterward; she'd always hated gulls and, anyway, why would anyone have allowed her to watch a TV marathon of Hitchcock movies the summer she was eleven, which, when all was said and done, had put an end to her love of birds; worse yet, Philomène was probably more frightened by her reaction than by the gull itself. "It's always the mother's fault," she hiccupped between two sobs, and Marion joked, "Yes, especially your mother, who let you watch *The Birds*," and the women smiled at each other; how nice it would be to put an end to the cycle of guilt, but it was like the weather or one season following on another, something that can't be reversed. In short, when, to lighten the mood, Julie suggested it was a perfect time for the men to go surfing, everyone had agreed, and Adam hadn't envisaged there could be any possible consequences to such a decision. How could he have known that less than an hour later, he'd have been tipped into a reality in appearance identical to the one he'd always known, but that would feel foreign and disturbing from that moment on?

He'd just about died and yet it just about hadn't happened, and everything he did now, every time he started up the car or chose a route between Hudson and his restaurant, Hudson and the TV studios, Hudson and Marion's clinic, every gulped-down meal or too-confident exit from the shower, every random move he made now held for him the weight of potential tragedy and he was powerless to do anything about it other than mulling it over non-stop because he hadn't spared a thought for the possibilities that day on the beach before the gull's attack and the surfing and the wave that he hadn't been able to outwit and Celia Smith's shattered knee.

"YOU LOOK LIKE DEATH WARMED OVER," CHANTALE SAID as Adam arrived at the studio to introduce *Adam à table*—the most popular cooking show on the most-viewed channel—for the station's fall launch. As she spoke, she tucked in her chin, creating a triple fold beneath a face that was usually slender, tanned, and youthful despite her fifty-four years, and Adam almost did the same out of sheer amazement; it was so surprising to see the features of such a fit woman transformed in such a radical way.

Was she pretty? It would seem so, that's what people wrote to her, day in and day out, beneath the pictures showing her devoting herself to the various wellness activities she liked to post on social media. *Too pretty, so pretty, are you ever pretty, look at how pretty you are, beautiful, stop, it's too much.* And it's true, she had hair that shone and a yogi's figure free of rough edges. Perhaps that was enough. Adam thought he might ask her whether she thought she was pretty. "Do you think you're pretty, Chantale?" Apparently, that's what counted. But he said nothing, didn't tuck in his chin, simply rubbed his right cheek, mopped a trickle of perspiration off his brow already cold from the studio's air conditioning, and thought how the expression *death warmed over* was downright alarming. To look like death warmed over, you had to be dead.

Dead and buried.

—
35

"Hey, Adam, it's just a joke," Chantale added, punching him in the arm (her ring with its infinity symbol scratching his mole, the one that looked like it had changed shape recently, don't you think, Marion?). "You're weird today."

Adam remembered that neither Chantale in media relations nor Richard in production nor Mathieu in development knew about the surfing accident: for that, he would have had to tell them, he would have had to be able to talk about it without sheer nausea rising to his uvula, and he had no intention of vomiting in front of the whole crew in the TV station that employed him, even less so only a few minutes before going on air. Adam stammered out an apology and made a hackneyed joke about the urgent need for coffee that active people experienced, and fled to the washroom pretending to answer a call on his cellphone.

He'd entered Marion's number. "My patient's almost frozen, I have two minutes," she warned him, and despite the lilt to her voice and her words uttered without a hint of impatience, Adam felt ridiculous for calling her, for disturbing her on the job, a genuine, humble job, repairing teeth, what could be more concrete? What could be more undeniably useful? While he did what? Made omelettes *à la sauge* in a luxurious kitchen rented at great expense to imitate his own luxurious kitchen? "I won't keep you long," he said, immediately regretting the hint of reproach in his voice; that wasn't what he wanted, to make Marion feel guilty, yet how could he deny it? His tone was so bitter it made his throat burn.

"What's going on?" Marion asked, ignoring his opening line, and this time there was no mistaking it: she was worried and full of solicitude. Not irritated, not put out.

His Marion, generous and all ears.

When he opened his mouth again, Adam was surprised to feel the damp of tears on his cheeks.

"I can't do the season launch."

"What do you mean?"

"I mean it won't be possible. It would mean me sitting in that chair, having my makeup done, waiting my turn to go on while making small talk with the others from children's shows and the news, joking about our respective holidays and making fun of the downy beard sported by Jean-Michel, who's hosting both the season launch and the evening talk show, and afterward I'll have to sit in the guest chair during the break and shake the hand of the host, who's been sweating for the past two hours, and I'll have to help him out, he needs it, Marion, because he's already sick of the whole shebang, he can't take it anymore, so he barely asks the question before we rush in, talking about our seventh season with whatever charisma we have left and saying that this year there'll be something new, this year we'll be targeting those who've turned their backs on cooking, singles, young people, too, so important to get young people excited, who knows, we might sow the seed for tomorrow's next great chef among them. We have to say all that and name the contributors and take the host's ribbing and, if possible, do a bit of our own, everyone teasing everyone else, Marion, and I don't think I can face it, I simply can't face all that today."

There was a brief silence on the other end of the line, barely long enough for Adam to catch his breath—it was as though Marion, too, had stopped breathing when he began speaking, not recognizing the words, who on earth talked like that? Not him, never. He used to love season launches, before. It was like the first day of school, he often told Marion, when you get to catch up with your friends and brag a bit.

"You used to love season launches," Marion said pensively, echoing what he'd heard in his own head. And her comment needled him. Did she understand nothing? A wall had just shot up between them, and he knew, without knowing why, that he would punish her for what she had just said.

"Sorry to have been a bother, I've got to go."

"But you're not a bo—"

He hung up and held onto the phone in the hollow of his damp hand, tight, as though to extract something—an answer— from it.

Over the sink, he splashed water onto his face, but the warmish, motion-activated jet dried up when his hand withdrew. He wiped his face with a brown paper towel, and its rough texture gave him a bit of respite: *The hurt confirms I'm alive*, he thought as he kept rubbing for a few more seconds till his temple turned red.

I'm okay, I'm okay, a great summer, I went to the seashore, a great time with the gang, lots of barbecues, you know me. Oh, no way could I get out of making ribs, and I'll have you know my recipe is still infallible, even on a camp stove and even under extreme conditions like my mother-in-law's convection oven! Correct, Jean-Michel, there is no excuse—anyone can cook ribs, that's my firmly held belief. Hahahahahaha. You'll have to come over to our place someday, I'll rescue you from your gastronomical doldrums, you've got to make your own sauce, seriously, ready-made sauces have had their day—other than mine, on sale in fine grocery stores, hahahahahaha. This year, we'll keep helping people acquire cooking skills with new menu plans and finds, there's Rita, our Italian queen, who'll accompany me, and together we'll promote even more local artisans, you know how crazy I am for local products. Hahahahahaha. Hahahahahaha, get on with you. There's never enough time to say all there is to say when you're around, but they say that's part of your charm—

Every Sunday at 5 p.m., that's right.

Thank you, Jean-Michel.

When he left the TV station, his shirt was drenched in sweat (he was glad he'd chosen navy blue) and he looked forward to the soothing autumn cool. He could congratulate himself on having trotted out the expected hype without faltering. But the month of August was nearing its end without any sign that summer, too, was drawing to a close, and he found himself cloaked in a dense layer of hot, cloying air in the time it took to walk from the entrance to his car. Once in the driver's seat, Adam said to himself, "I will lay my forehead down on this steering wheel and cry."

Which he did.

# 4

JESSIE WOULD OFTEN TRY TO INVITE MARION OUT FOR lunch, just the two of them, and every time Marion thought it was sweet of her, then said how great it would be, really great, but not today, too much paperwork, a quick trip to the esthetician's, another to the bank, but soon, for sure, I can't wait. She had trouble explaining the impulse that spurred her to turn down every invitation to lunch. She liked her assistant a lot, after all, always polite with the patients, a smiling young woman with no tendency to complain the way Virginie, her former assistant, used to. Jessie tried again after the holidays, singing the praises of the wonderful jar salads she'd learned to make over the summer, and she proposed a noon hour when they'd both be free (Tuesday in ten days' time). Having run out of excuses, Marion agreed.

So now, on a Tuesday ten days later, she found herself sitting with Jessie on one of the benches that had recently been installed in the small park by the clinic. City council had decided to go all out to impress urbanites willing to leave the downtown core. Water features in modern colours, park benches made of perforated metal, puny trees offering the promise of shade for the picnic blankets to come, everything here believing in the future.

"Anyway, we're thinking a winter wedding so I can wear a stole, but Kevin doesn't like the idea as much. He keeps saying, 'What will people do with their boots?' It bugs him, and I have to admit he's got a point there," Jessie explained as she opened the Mason jars; her wonderful salads in coloured layers, vinaigrette on the side, delighted and surprised Marion, surprise that was immediately followed by a touch of remorse. Who was she to be astonished to see an assistant make such— her first thought was *refined*—let's say, contemporary salads? On top of it all, they were delicious, with their cumin-infused pumpkin seeds and a hint of ginger in the vinaigrette.

"What did you have," Jessie was asking, "a winter or summer wedding?"

Marion smiled. "I'm not married, but if I did marry, it would be in the fall, in an orchard, at the end of apple season. I grew up in Oka—I suppose there's no escaping it."

The words came of their own accord, as though she'd answered the same question many times before when not only had it never been asked, but she herself had never given it any thought. Yet her answer came without hesitation, a certainty. Any knowledge she'd been blind to always disturbed her somewhat: What else did she know about herself? Jessie's eyes, made up with care (her doe eyes made her look like a rockabilly pin-up star), widened.

"I was positive you two were married," she responded, her voice mildly troubled. "You've been together for so long!"

Had they really been together *for so long?* Marion supposed that, from a twenty-four-year-old's standpoint, their time together represented a century. The ten years had gone by extraordinarily quickly, almost treacherously, insidiously so, and had carried away her thirties, forcing her to brave her forties unprepared and, above all, with not much to show in the way of results: no children, essentially. What other requirement had such a strict deadline? There'd always be time to take a trip around the world or to become a real *powerhouse* someday. Or to marry. You can marry at ninety years of age. Or never.

Jessie proceeded to give a detailed account of the menu she envisaged for the reception; she wanted a chocolate cake yet didn't know if she could have chocolate on chocolate or whether she should make do with a chocolate sponge cake topped with white icing. "A white cake is a surer bet, but chocolate is my life," she added. "We won't tell our patients, though." She gave a conspiratorial laugh. Marion suddenly understood that Jessie considered her to be a friend, or at least that Jessie wanted to be her friend, and the idea, rather than seeming an honour, which was her usual feeling when others showed any sign of interest, felt intrusive, and she had a quick image of her grabbing Jessie by the shoulders and pushing her into the park's central basin.

She did nothing of the sort, of course, and felt so ashamed afterward that she said if Jessie would like, she could look for the perfect cake with her and even ask Adam for his opinion. Jessie's eyes grew moist, and, with flushed cheeks, she whispered how very kind, she couldn't believe it, which made Marion grimace despite herself.

She started to regret having accepted the lunch invitation, and the mouthfuls of quinoa, grated carrot, and watercress began to make her feel sick. She stopped eating, and Jessie worried it might be the salad. Marion was quick to reassure her, saying the salad was delicious, but she'd had too much for breakfast, Adam had made French toast, and how could anyone resist Adam's French toast?

That wasn't true. Adam made nothing these days, he spent the first hour every morning staring at the field behind the house. From time to time, he'd interrupt the stillness with the words "Goddamn high-voltage wire."

At first, Marion thought he just needed time to get over the goddamn wire and move on to something else as he always did when a new project came along. But now, enough was enough, and she no longer knew whether to turn a blind eye to his obsession and bury the wire at huge expense or to tell Adam that all his talk was getting on her nerves.

"He makes you breakfast every morning? Lucky you," Jessie was saying, a dreamy look in her eye, perhaps imagining the married life that awaited her, the couple's complicity, the fair and continuous exchange of favours: she'd look after the groceries, and he'd make risotto; she'd bear children, and he'd take them skating. She will give him hard-ons, and he will give her orgasms. And later, when they are old and wrinkled and dressed with somewhat outdated elegance, they will sit together on the couch holding hands, and through the throat-clearing and fits of coughing from their worn-out lungs, they will tell each other that their life has met their every expectation because it was spent together. Oh, there will have been trials, of course, cold shoulders and wars of nerves, but they won't dwell on those because the minute each trial shows up in the rear-view mirror, it loses its shape, joins the others, forms a sort of magma—familiar, inert, almost comforting—and even though they are bound to come up, there's no desire to talk about them. Who wants to hear the repeated whack of life's disappointments?

Marion inhaled abruptly and fastened the lid back onto the salad container. Then flashed a broad smile, which wasn't even hard to summon. "Kevin is pretty wonderful himself, hon, and I think you two will have a fabulous life." She had no idea whether or not she was lying.

ADÈLE RARELY EXPRESSED THE DESIRE TO SPEND AN EVEning with her father, so when Adam's daughter called her on her cell, Marion, busy hardening a patient's amalgam, picked up immediately to be sure Adèle didn't change her mind.

"Nonsense, I'll come fetch you," she was quick to reply when Adèle half-heartedly offered to take public transit. The drive represented a considerable detour for Marion, but was nothing but an inconvenience since it meant not having Adèle change her mind and send them a laconic text message along the lines of *something came up, we'll do it some other time, (sry)*, accompanied by a sad-looking yellow face with an oversized tear. Plus, Adam had been so strange lately, beginning with the nonsensical phone call she'd received from him the day of his season launch. Marion had never figured out what he was asking her for or even whether he had been asking her for anything at all.

Usually, what he wanted from her was simple: words of encouragement, *I believe in you, you're the best*, arguments in favour of the viewpoint he wanted to put forward—or, when she felt brave, in favour of one she felt was better—and a readiness to listen at all times.

That day, on the phone, as she trotted out the usual—and since she couldn't lay her hand on the back of his neck, she adopted an even gentler tone of voice, not too gentle, Adam wouldn't want her to pity him, no one likes that—he kept repeating things to himself as though she weren't even there; she had no hold on him. Then he'd hung up and had given no other sign of life till evening. She'd called him back numerous times to no avail. He must have turned off his phone during the taping and forgotten to turn it back on. That was plausible. But it wasn't like him. Making her way to their house down the winding, tree-lined lane that had always brought her a feeling of relief, *Here, finally, I'm safe*, she caught sight of Adam's car parked at the end. If he was back, everything must be all right, mustn't it? Yet he hadn't turned his phone back on.

She opened the door cautiously, as though to the accompaniment of an ominous soundtrack of sustained cello notes. She wanted to call out to Adam, but her dry mouth made it impossible and so she kept quiet. With lights off, the house sat in what was ordinarily a pleasant half-light sculpted by the swaying of the trees on the other side of the windows, one consistent with the chalky white of the walls, a colour that seemed to absorb all sound, so downy its hue; in any case, that's what their designer had said in choosing it.

That night, however, the branches cast lugubrious shadows on surfaces, as though sending an ill omen. Slowly, Marion walked to the end of the hallway and to their bedroom in its independent wing.

"So we never have to worry about making too much noise," Adam had said, "even when the children are here."

Marion had refrained from saying that, given the frequency of their visits, it wouldn't make much of a difference; however, his dream had been to have his own wing, an idea he found eminently sexy, and Marion had no desire to talk about the children anymore.

That was where she found him, clothed and sound asleep on their bed. He was snoring the way he did after a bender, but didn't smell of alcohol. She shut the door again and walked to the bathroom—not the ensuite, but the one for guests. She turned on the taps and shoved her head beneath the spray of cold water without really knowing what fire she was extinguishing. An hour later, he got up, starving, and made pasta.

When she asked him how he was doing, he said fine, fine, it went just fine, after all, sorry to have bothered you.

Ever since, Adam's napping had increased and Marion had trouble getting used to it.

Now she sat waiting for Adèle in front of her home. A classic duplex of the thirties, Sarah's house made a fine impression on its small residential street with its original stained glass and never-painted oak door. Perhaps the former home of a notary. Or a doctor. Marion didn't like to remind herself that it had once been Adam's home. Not that she had a particularly possessive personality or envied the house itself, but the thought made her picture the interlaced bodies of Adam and his ex, and that she didn't like. Adam had always spoken of Sarah with a certain detached respect, the way you speak of a female cousin or a music teacher who'd made it possible for you to learn how to play a bit of guitar round a campfire—Sarah had given him two beautiful children and had been accommodating when he'd needed it. He appreciated her fortitude and yet never missed an opportunity to tell Marion how much Sarah's bad moods and fondness for television had killed any eroticism between them.

Shortly after he and Marion met, he told Marion about the time he'd wanted to make love to Sarah while she was watching a soap opera about the tribulations of a group of crazy young doctors, and how she'd said, "Go ahead, but don't block my view."

That anecdote, meant to reassure Marion about the chasm separating their own sex life from the one he'd had with Sarah, had had the opposite effect. Marion concluded that, back then, Adam had desired Sarah. That he had kneaded her breasts and slapped her ass, something he liked to do to give a rhythm to the moment and leave a trace on her body, a red mark that said, *Adam was here.* He'd tongue-kissed her and maybe even pulled her hair. She'd put his penis in her mouth.

Today, as she waved at Sarah from her car window and as Adèle walked down the three steps off the front porch, it was hard to believe that all that had ever taken place. As for Sarah, did the same images play in her head? Did she say to herself, *Huh, this is the woman who sometimes receives on her belly the sperm of the man who used to come on me, this is the woman with whom I share that experience.* Did she find it as strange as Marion did?

Adèle shut the car door and immediately rolled down her window. "Arggh, what's that smell?"

In a patient tone, Marion replied that she herself didn't smell anything in particular, but, given her sensitivity to odours, Adèle must detect something that didn't reach other people's nostrils.

"Nothing subtle about this stench," Adèle scoffed, and Marion smiled.

"Okay, sorry, I must smell like the clinic, I'll open my window, too."

Marion drove north, hoping the Métropolitaine wouldn't be too congested, a pointless wish as always. It would take them over an hour to drive to Hudson, and if ever there had been periods when she longed for time alone with Adèle to cement their affection outside of their respective relationships with Adam, she'd since seen how difficult it was to hold an actual conversation with her stepdaughter, so the idea of finding herself in a Montreal traffic jam with Adèle made her even more nervous. That's what it all came down to: her eighteen-year-old stepdaughter made her nervous. A brilliant and blasé student, she'd always had a phenomenal ability to heap contempt on teachers in elementary school, whom she deemed mediocre, then in high school and now in CEGEP. Everything was fodder for criticism: the texts they used, their language tics, and even their breathing habits. It was the misfortune of one math teacher she'd had to suffer from chronic rhinitis, which Adèle sniggered over with her friends, recording and texting the frequency with which he sniffled in class: *today at intervals of twelve seconds, yesterday sixteen, when do we reach the ten-second mark?* Adam didn't like it when his daughter showed that side of her personality, which reminded him of Sarah's—intransigent and unfair. "Marion, it's as though I disappoint her every time I open my mouth," Adam whispered one evening when Adèle offered a few scathing remarks about her school principal, describing his use of *anyways,* with its unnecessary *s* at the end, as being *punishable by death.* Whenever Adam intervened, his daughter acknowledged his interruption with such coldness that, generally speaking, he simply smiled and ran a hand through her hair, thick and coppery like his own.

"Daughter of mine, you'll rule the planet someday," he'd say, and although generic comments of the sort usually elicited a string of zingers from Adèle, her father's approval must have meant enough to disarm her, and she'd return his smile.

Marion didn't have the same status in Adèle's eyes. "How is it being back at school?" was all Marion asked, scanning the road. An unmoving eighteen-wheeler ahead blocked her view. It had Alberta licence plates and sported the bumper sticker GOD IS MY CO-PILOT. Cars in the right lane weren't moving any faster, and Marion concluded there was no point trying to pass the truck.

"Do you have good teachers?"

Adèle shrugged without looking at her. "They're okay."

Marion bobbed her head up and down a tad too long as she cast round for an answer that never came. Adèle pointed at the truck.

"I saw a meme of a car after a big crash, like its hood was flattened, its body crushed, the windshield shattered. It had a licence plate like that sticker, you know, the plates you screw on the front? *God is my co-pilot.* Looks like God had had it with you, moron."

Marion laughed.

Adèle pursed her lips. "It's not that funny." She spoke almost to herself, as though she felt guilty hearing Marion's laughter fill the interior of the car.

"Sometimes they're too in-your-face with their conservative views," Marion retorted. "It feels good to vent a little, that's all."

The cars started moving again, and Marion was relieved to have something to do. Was this a good time to discuss Adam's mood with Adèle? Probably not. He himself refused to talk about it, and Marion had decided to fall back on the tried and true—and tacit—approach of safety-valve sex at evening's end, and a long hug in the morning standing in the kitchen, her elbows glued to Adam's side, her palms on the shoulder blades of the man who used to hold himself tall ten years ago and who now stood with a stoop as though forever toting heavy grocery bags in each hand. In any event, how would she even explain to Adèle what was going on?

Your father collided with a girl off the beach and swallowed water and may have pinched a nerve in his neck, nothing dramatic or tangibly serious, unlike for the girl, oh, the girl, a dislocated knee and most likely a torn anterior cruciate ligament, she'll be dealing with it for years, we don't know much more about her condition, she didn't leave her contact information, her name is Celia Smith and we know almost nothing about her, however, what we do know is that after it happened, Adam cried and cried at the sight of the knee, not his, his knees had barely a scrape, no, the girl's, seeing the girl's knee, he cried, loud, high-pitched sobs, like those of the children you hear in the distance in the playground when they've fallen off the swing or when their parents are forcing them to go home for bedtime, sobs of despair. I still don't know if his tears came from pain or fear or guilt or disgust, but I can tell you, Adèle, that I haven't had the courage to ask and risk seeing him start sobbing all over again, I can't, I just can't, Adèle, because part of me feels like the man I've loved for the past ten years ceased to exist off Lucy Vincent Beach on Martha's Vineyard and that I've brought back to Quebec the empty shell of a man, his ectoplasm, and that the rest of him, *his very matter*, washed up on the sand and was carried away by the tide and today floats somewhere off an island in the Atlantic, Nantucket, with any luck, the Bermuda Triangle more likely, and I've felt so alone, Adèle, so alone and so furious, for longer than I care to admit.

No, she couldn't say that.

Marion turned up the volume on the radio and followed as best she could a cultural reporter's enthusiastic, over-the-top account of her visit to an exhibit on the newly discovered sarcophagus of a pharaoh almost as well-known as Tutankhamun whose relics, loaned out by some museum from somewhere in Europe, were extraordinarily well-preserved; it was a must-see, a perfect family outing since even the little ones would find something of interest, in any case, her children had loved the

51

trip and taken part in the crafts workshop making mummy bandages out of papier-mâché in the museum's young people's space, which, did you know, Martine, was renovated recently and offers weekly workshops, each more fascinating than the last? What a wonderful opportunity to turn off our screens and expand our culture at the museum! she enthused over the car's speakers. Adèle gave a dry little laugh that sounded more like a cat's sneeze, and Marion felt a wave of such tenderness for her and such weariness in the face of the world that she just about let go of the steering wheel to enfold her in her arms, hug her close and tell her, "I love you, Adèle, I love you despite everything, I will always love you."

But she didn't.

# 5

AT THE WHEEL OF HIS LAND ROVER, ADAM FOLLOWED THE
car driven by the real estate agent who, in turn, was tailing
Sylvain Sweet's pickup to the house that belonged to his
father, Gerry Sweet, a maple sugar producer on the cusp of
retiring and the owner of a maple sugar stand he hoped to sell.
She wouldn't let an opportunity like this slip through her fingers. Without exerting too much pressure, she had to encourage
her clients to make an offer as quickly as possible before doubt
undermined their enthusiasm. Obviously, her method didn't
always work and many potential buyers withdrew from a
transaction, invoking all kinds of nebulous reasons, but sometimes her zeal paid off—not to mention that, when a client as
prestigious as Adam Dumont asked to visit one of your list-
ings, you had to jump at the opportunity.

"We could have some tea and sign the papers at your house,
what do you think, Mr. Sweet?" she'd said a bit too loudly, and
Adam suspected she always spoke to seniors that way, with a
combination of solicitude and condescension, as though they
were foolish yet endearing animals.

In the next breath, she said something she'd already trotted out twice before, "What a great name, given what you do! How incredible, being a Sweet who makes maple syrup! It was meant to be!"

And Mr. Sweet Sr.—she confidently called Sylvain by his first name—smiled and nodded.

"'Sweets for my sweet,' my wife said when we met. It's a song we used to listen to back then. 'Sweets for my sweet, sugar for my honey, your tasty lips please me so.'"

He stopped singing, interrupted by a hacking fit. Sylvain patted him on the back, much too lightly to clear his father's airway, but that wasn't his goal, Adam supposed, surprised to be so deeply moved by such an ordinary gesture.

The agent felt it a fitting moment to exclaim, "Don't choke quite yet, Mr. Sweet, we haven't been to see the notary yet," and Adam was sorry it was too late for Sylvain and him to come to an agreement on their own and avoid having to listen any further to the woman's prattle. Since his intention was to offer the asking price, he could hope that their association would be short-lived.

It only took them a few minutes to reach the house, a trip the Sweets often made by tractor. It was a small farmhouse from the late nineteenth century that would have had hemlock siding originally, but had succumbed to the aluminum-siding wave of the sixties. The facing on the Sweets' home was white verging on grey, dotted here and there with green moss. Although not neglected, the house was not particularly pretty either, and its windows of guillotine metal must surely pinch fingers as they were being closed. Adam wondered when the hardware from the original windows, the espagnolette locks or half-moon-shaped handles, had been removed. The wood must have rotted, and, having compared the cost of restoring them with the cost of new windows, the Sweet family mustn't have hesitated.

Adam parked behind the agent and followed the group inside. Sylvain had them sit at the dining room table and offered them tea, coffee, and water as well as a couple of cans of ginger ale. The agent refused politely, Adam accepted a glass of water, and Mr. Sweet said nothing. A few minutes later, his son set a small cup of steaming tea in front of him, either orange or spice, Adam couldn't quite tell.

"Mr. Dumont would like to make a promise to purchase right away. That's always good news since it's an expression of keen interest," the agent explained.

Sylvain nodded, saying it was music to their ears, but Gerry gave a grunt that soon turned into a coughing fit, to which his son responded by ordering, "Take a sip of tea, Papa."

"We've already had other offers that went nowhere," the old man said finally, after wetting his lips with some tea. "We'll believe it when we see it."

Adam shook his head. "I understand, Mr. Sweet. Rest assured that my mind is made up. Owning my own sugar maple stand is a long-held dream. I was too busy these last few years to do anything about it, but ever since my first restaurant, I've always wanted to grow some of the products I serve to my customers. The farm-to-table experience and local production are real values of mine. I live nearby, I catch the ferry in Hudson and, before you know it, in twenty minutes I'm here. My partner was born in Oka; this is our home. This is our home."

Also, if you don't mind me saying so, I just about died this summer and ever since I've had trouble sleeping; I fall asleep exhausted, wake up with a start, terrified, on the verge of drowning, my heart racing, and turn to Marion lying next to me and am acutely aware of the finite nature of things, the impermanence of any possible serenity, and that observation hurts, Mr. Sweet, Sylvain, that observation cuts me to the quick, and sometimes I cry, me, the man who only used to cry at touching or sad movies—it's normal, healthy, to cry then, it proves you're no psychopath—but these tears, these new tears, are different, they wash nothing away, and there's no feeling better afterward, instead you've got a headache and a stuffy nose and a panic-stricken feeling that you'll never feel okay again and you're sorry you didn't enjoy the good times enough, and you promise yourself that, if ever someday you should feel better, you'll enjoy everything to the full, oh yes, you'll dive into that life of sunsets and pancake breakfasts. The only advantage to these new tears is that they eventually run out and you fall asleep again—only to wake up fifteen minutes later to have everything start all over again. That's what it's like almost every night, Mr. Sweet, Sylvain, and the problem is that no matter how much you want to find joy again, it's not easy when you're not sleeping at night, a minor detail no one talks about, but sleep is an absolute prerequisite for a feeling of well-being, yet without that feeling you have a hard time fall-ing asleep, and without sleep you have trouble finding that feeling, it's what's called a vicious circle, as you know, I know you know, we all know, but let me tell you, it's something else entirely when you figure that out. What I mean is that when

I stood on your dirt road earlier under the blue tubing between the maple trees, and a gust of wind set the leaves to rustling and the cedar waxwings to squawking, I felt joy, real joy, and thought: This is the path forward, I will make way for joy.

Adam didn't say all that. Actually, he stopped after the bit about his girlfriend born in Oka. "This is home," Adam said, then he branched off to talk about his passion for maple products, a more complex, denser sugar than white sugar. On TV, it was the specials on maple products that evoked the most passion. Maple involved so much more than a banal agricultural commodity, it was a strong symbol of our identity, and did you know that the crème brûlée from DNA's menu made with maple syrup from Quebec had won over the president of France during his last visit here?

Sylvain smiled listening to him, nodding frequently, while his father simply stirred a spoonful of sugar—white sugar— into his teacup. All of a sudden, Adam felt like a fool, the back of his neck began to burn and his pulse sped up: a panic attack was about to strike. He had to take the plunge. "I'm offering the exact amount asked for, with no conditions other than this one, perhaps: Sylvain, would you be willing to keep working the land and give me a hand? I'm known to offer very competitive wages to the people who work with me."

The agent, mentally primed for an extended period of hard bargaining, blinked once, speechless. Mr. Sweet set his spoon down by his cup.

"You're not pulling our chain, are you?" he said, unsmiling.

Adam shook his head. "I've never been more serious in my life."

—

Sylvain let out a long sigh, then laughed. "This is our dream scenario, isn't it, Papa? Remember when we put the maple stand up for sale, I said, 'Papa, the dream scenario would be to have someone buy it and take me on, that way we'd still have money coming in but no stress, then you could retire at last.' Do you remember, that's what I said and you said, you said, 'Son, stop daydreaming, we'll be lucky if we sell in two years after knocking the price down,' but sometimes it does happen, sometimes good things do happen, huh, Papa?"

STEPPING INTO HIS CAR ONCE HE'D FILLED OUT THE REQUI-site papers, Adam saw that Marion had left a message earlier that afternoon. Adèle was coming for supper, Marion would pick her up on her way home, and they'd probably have to tell her to take the train back to the city or encourage her to spend the night at their place, which Adèle wouldn't appreciate, but it would probably make more sense because she herself would be too tired to drive late at night and she felt he, too, needed a rest, in short, she wasn't trying to be mean, she might still have enough energy to drive Adèle home after supper, in fact, who knows, there was no point deciding ahead of time, forget what I just said, honey, I'm thinking out loud, I'm always so happy to have her over.

It was then that Adam realized he had just committed to buying and operating a sugar maple stand flanked by a small growing orchard for $750,000 plus tax without even consulting Marion.

ADÈLE SAID SHE WASN'T VERY HUNGRY, WHICH ADAM KNEW to be untrue. As a child, she had been curious, enthusiastic, happy to follow her father into the restaurant's kitchen to taste sauces, tartars, and rare vegetables. Since her teen years, the trend had been the opposite. First, at the age of thirteen, she declared she was a vegetarian. That her father, known province-wide for his specialty, a new take on braised pork, took this as a disavowal didn't seem to affect either his daughter or Sarah, who boasted about Adèle's moral qualities and, let's say it, her courage, we were nowhere near as committed at her age, you should admire her more than anything.

As for Marion, she comforted Adam by saying, "You can still make her your cheese soufflé that she adores."

Which Adam did, preparing as many cheese soufflés as there were visits from Adèle that year, until she announced her intolerance to lactose. At fourteen, she developed an aversion to root vegetables. At fifteen, it was fried foods that gave her gas. At sixteen, she turned down the chocolate praline cake he'd baked for her birthday, earning him an annoyed call from Sarah: he knew how sugar made her migraines worse! Yet, he'd watch her gobble down one bowl of cereal after another the minute she arrived at their place, and you'd have had to have a full-blown cold not to catch the scent of fries from the McDonald's at Central Station when she came by train. Adam understood nothing but the evidence: the only aversion his daughter had was to anything made by her father. Through her repeated refusals—which she now couched in the basic cour-tesies that adults fell back on, "I'm not hungry" instead of "it's no good"—Adèle communicated something primordial to him: she forbade him entry into her world, punishing him either for his absences or because he'd left her mother, or because she thought him to be a moron. She refused to have him feed her because he had never known how. At least, that was what Marion suggested on evenings when she gave in to the desire to analyze the situation. "The best you can do, honey, is to keep loving her, but not let her run roughshod over you. We offer her what we've made, say nothing if she doesn't eat it, and so refuse to feed the beast, if you'll excuse the expression."

Adam nodded; Marion was right. As he liked to say, Marion was almost always right, and whenever he disagreed, it was more on principle: their conversations had to be fuelled by something. Even so, every time he set down in front of his daughter a plateful of spaghetti carbonara (no lardons or cream), a stew of curried vegetables flavoured with lemongrass, Tonkinese soup, grilled eggplant topped with vegan yogourt and pomegranate seeds, homemade squash-and-sage-butter ravioli, bibimbap, avocado maki, dinner crepes (albeit one of her childhood favourites), a lentil shepherd's pie, a Provençal tart, a ratatouille, and she said for the thousandth time, "Thanks, but I'm not very hungry," before devouring half a container of cookies-and-cream ice cream from the freezer, he felt like slapping her.

That evening was devoted to leftovers, and Adèle would just have to make do—or not. Running late due to signing the promise to purchase and an unusually high ridership on the Oka-Hudson ferry, Adam let Marion look after it all. When he arrived, the table was overflowing with delicious traces of earlier meals: grilled peppers, slow-roasted tomatoes, tzatziki, flatbread, arugula pesto, cheeses, dried sausage, a Purslane lettuce from the garden, and, for Adam, Korean-style strips of marinated flank steak.

"How about we do a sandwich bar?" she asked, opening a bottle of wine and offering her cheek to Adam for a kiss.

"Sounds perfect," Adam replied, "you're perfect," and Marion flashed a strained—or was it ambivalent?—smile. Did she guess he'd been up to something?

Adèle turned down the cheeses, accepted a glass of wine (one of the rare things they agreed on now that she was of drinking age, their mutual snobbery in favour of organic wines), and nibbled on salted pistachios, piling the shells up on the table despite the small bowl Marion had provided for that specific purpose only ten centimetres away.

"Uh, I was wondering if I could get my Christmas gift early this year," Adèle blurted out before running her tongue over her eyetooth to dislodge a piece of pistachio.

Adam and Marion looked at one another: so this was the reason for her visit.

"Only 'cause I'd like to go to Thailand this winter, but if you don't buy the plane tickets in advance, it gets really expensive."

For a few years now, Félix and Adèle had each received a thousand dollars on their birthdays and at Christmas in the form of a cheque signed by their father. Where Félix conscientiously saved his money for large purchases—a car, a watch, now a condo—the same money slipped through Adèle's fingers. No one could figure out how she ended up with a bank balance of zero only a few months later, given that her parents paid all her expenses.

"Thailand? Wouldn't that mean you'd miss part of your semester at CEGEP?"

Adèle shrugged, annoyed. "Says the former model student," she hissed sarcastically.

"Oh, I just remembered, we have a bit of hummus, too," Marion said. "Would you like me to wash some carrots to go with it?"

Adam laid his hand over hers, as though to say, Leave it be, don't overcompensate for her spitefulness, we've lost in advance, leave it be, as long as we're together, I'm happy, even though that wasn't true, together or not, Adam was no longer happy, and tonight it was more acute than ever, scarcely two hours ago he'd been walking through the woods with the Sweet father and son and had thought to himself, *This is it, this is it, I've found it*, and now nothing was certain anymore; he wondered whether a $750,000 hole in their savings was reasonable, whether he should continue in the same vein, buying his children's esteem with money; he now saw with extraordinary clarity that Adèle would never love him, that he would inevitably disappoint Marion, that people would tire of him, of his restaurants and his TV shows, that eventually he would close down and sink into oblivion. Knowing that, he'd do better to jealously guard his fortune and have it fructify by investing in the safest instruments for his future since he would always suffer and he had to at least make sure he would suffer *comfortably*, prostrate, his face averted from the window, his palms over his ears, beyond reach and in the dark till the end of time.

Then Gerry Sweet's sickly features appeared before him and he knew he would not back down.

# 6

CHOIR REHEARSALS WERE HELD ON MONDAY EVENINGS IN the community centre next to the path leading to the municipal beach, and Marion decided she'd jog through the woods on her way there. After all, it was her day off.

For years, patients had asked for the clinic to stay open on Saturdays, a change Claude was hell-bent on resisting. There was the chalet and the golf foursome and the cycling clubs and, really, no, people could just work round it; did anyone ask them to work Saturdays to accommodate someone else? Marion steered clear of the discussion; once she had tried to tell him that, actually, a lot of people did work on Saturdays, in particular those who looked after him at the golf course and the service station and the restaurant, and he'd seemed hurt at the accusation of insensitivity. Marion felt guilty, and he may have exploited that, yes, he had taken advantage of Marion's tendency to feel guilt, and he was quick to suggest that she, Marion, should take over on Saturdays if she thought it was all that important.

So she'd agreed, out of principle, out of kindness. Out of cowardice. In return, she'd declared she would take Mondays off, and the arrangement turned out to be more enjoyable than she'd imagined it would be.

She was free to stroll through the small city's streets, deserted now yet bustling on weekends. She walked along the winding roads to the centre of Hudson, sometimes popping into shops full of candles and flowery decorative articles, caftans made of raw silk, and knick-knacks painted in the colours of the English flag. The sense of affinity with England was strong in Hudson, and if, on Sundays, the antiquated charm of cyclists wearing tweed caps, pedal pushers, and the lace-up brown leather shoes of rural folk from the between-war years delighted Marion, their allegiance to the British Empire did surprise her somewhat. She had hoped that Hudson, Quebec, would be a reflection of Hudson, New York: progressive, into organic food, wine bars, independent bookstores with an aroma of wood and intelligence, which was in part the case where food and good coffee were concerned. Yet there remained a whiff of conservatism akin to the fragrance infused by a balsam fir mist that failed to conceal a dusty essence. Marion didn't like to entertain negative thoughts about her city, and she kept from doing so by actively clinging to anything that could help her believe that reality matched—surpassed, even—the dream.

That desire is what led her to sign up to audition for the choir with the English name Hudson Hopefuls, an amateur group made up of people from the surrounding area. Their sporadic performances in the region—here to sing Christmas carols on a snowy street corner a few days before the holidays, there to give a benefit concert in the fight against homophobia—constituted in Marion's view one of the city's most significant assets. The choir included a few grey-hairs and two or three bald heads, but for the most part, the singers were in their thirties or early forties and managed businesses or careers as visual artists while raising a troupe of children with names like Piper, Poet, and Pearl. They exuded open-mindedness and solicitude for their community, and Marion wanted only one thing: to trade knowing glances with them.

The choir director was a short man who blushed easily and was prone to self-derision. Patrick still had the reddish-blond locks of his childhood, and, behind his metal-rimmed glasses, his eyes shone with an irresistible, joyful sparkle. As he conducted, the singers' motions followed their director's, he on tiptoe, bouncing, then swaying from side to side when the music slowed. Adam had noticed Marion's delighted smile when they went to the choir's jazz recital for Valentine's Day and told her that she should sing with them since she was always humming a tune or going on about the golden days of her high school choir. Marion laughed, it was a joke, but the idea grew on her. One morning, as Adam again kept to his bed after a restless night, Marion went out for a run and saw, on the outdoor message board at the community centre, an announcement for auditions.

She sang "I've Got a Crush on You," shakily but in tune. Two weeks and one phone call later, she'd made the cut.

"*Je pense tu vas avoir du fun avec nous autres,*" Patrick had said in the halting, singsong French of a bilingual Anglophone, and Marion hoped she'd have fun with them, too.

At the first rehearsal, she didn't have time for a run beforehand as she'd planned. She was about to leave when she heard a revving noise outside. A big mower, or a boat, maybe? Walking down the lane, she realized the noise was coming from a chainsaw in the woods separating their house from the road. Their woods. Marion followed the sound till she caught sight of Adam starting into the trunk of an old pine, one of the biggest trees on their lot.

She called his name—"Adam!"—three times before he heard and switched off the saw.

"What are you doing?"

"Don't worry, it's just a little cleanup."

"That's our biggest tree, it's almost a hundred years old. You don't just decide to cut down a hundred-year-old tree like that. If it falls the wrong way, you could get hurt."

"Stop making it into such a big deal."

"Adam, this is crazy."

"What's crazy is that damn wire. Even crazier, the way you refuse to see how it totally ruins our view."

Marion closed her eyes for a moment. The wire, of course. If he wasn't talking about it, he was staring at it through the window, grinding his teeth, fists clenched, prepping for a ridiculous showdown.

"Are you planning to knock the wire down by felling a few trees?"

"Seriously, what do you take me for? A fool?"

At first, Marion said nothing. Although she might not take him for a fool, neither was she prepared to state that he was acting like a sane person. What did she take him for then? Stunned at her failure to respond, Adam returned to the task at hand.

"Adam!"

Once again, he lowered the saw.

"I'm cutting the tree down to clear the ground, that way when we've buried the wire, we won't have to pay a pruner on top of the other expenses, that's all."

"Bury the wire? You don't even know if that's allowed!"

"Can I not do the least little thing without you watching over my every move, recording everything I do? You're not my boss, you know."

"Arghh. I refuse to speak to you when you get like this."

"In any case, I'll have possession of my land in a week, and you won't have me underfoot anymore. Over there, no one will try to tell me what to do."

Marion frowned. What land was he talking about? Had he lost touch with reality? Maybe things were worse than she'd imagined.

But Adam sighed and Marion detected neither aggressivity nor confusion there. It was a sorry, guilty sigh: a getting-ready-to-confess sigh. He came up to her and looked her in the eye.

"I'm really sorry. This isn't at all the way I wanted to tell you."

BY THE TIME MARION WALKED INTO THE COMMUNITY centre, the rehearsal had already begun. It was the start of a new season and they were all busy catching up on each other's news; here a joke about one couple's especially tough summer devoted to renovations, there the detailed account of a trip through the Greek islands, not the biggest ones where tourists disembarked in droves, but the small ones, beyond the Cyclades, where the ferry doesn't travel as often and where there's only one restaurant, yes, total bliss, and you're right, the kids loved it.

The obvious camaraderie among the choir members terrified Marion even as it made it possible for her to make a discreet entrance. What was she doing here? Adam had just announced that he'd bought a maple stand where he planned to spend his free time, Adam had just blown a fortune on a precarious plan, Adam had wanted this thing in secret, then acted in secret, then kept that secret for weeks. What was she doing here given the uneasy feeling she had that she no longer knew which way was north?

Marion turned on her heel and started to head for the door, coming face to face with Patrick, a platter of oatmeal cookies in his hands.

"Sweetie pie," he hummed, a nod to the song Marion sang for her audition, and she felt herself blush. If, on top of everything else, he was making fun of her, she had yet another reason to leave.

"*Biscuits!*" he announced, holding the platter out to her. "*Pour après.* People here are too focused on breaks and not enough on the music."

He had a smile on his face and no hint of reproach in his voice. "Come on, I'll introduce you to the others."

As she followed Patrick, Marion noticed that the skin of his scalp beneath his pale hair was an inflamed red. She recognized the same psoriasis scars her father had, the ones she'd glimpse beneath his shirt collar. Her grandfather had had the same scars under his mechanic's coveralls, and in his house the bathroom smelled of camphor oil, an odour Marion would always associate with peeling, painful skin. Patrick set the cookies down on a folding table by the piano, clapped twice with surprising authority, and the group dispersed quite naturally, everyone taking a seat without, however, stopping their chatter and laughter.

*The ease these people have with each other makes me want to experience the same,* Marion thought.

She wasn't used to expressing desires so clearly and felt embarrassed, almost paralyzed, as though afraid she'd spoken out loud. That wasn't the case. Patrick showed her where to sit, next to a woman in a bright red wool turtleneck and a yellow beret. Her placid smile heightened the colourful look, making her seem like a doll, a toy or, yes, a Lego lady.

"Hey, I'm Judy," the woman said in English, holding out her hand.

Marion gave her name and the woman immediately switched to French. There was no need to, not only was Marion's English quite good, but she was happy to use it, it gave her an opportunity—one she didn't often take advantage of, admittedly—to create another persona for herself, more daring, funnier, too. But she didn't know how to say so without making Judy feel her French wasn't good enough, so she said nothing.

Patrick announced that the Christmas concert would be held on December 7 in the Anglican church, eliciting a murmur of approval among those gathered there. Marion didn't know which of Hudson's churches was the Anglican one, she supposed it was the prettiest one, a small red-brick building with white wooden doors situated on a hillock surrounded by willow trees.

"Did you tell them half the choir is gay?" the tenor cried. "We wouldn't want to bring on any heart attacks."

Everyone laughed, then Patrick began the warm-up, striking a chord on the piano. The choir stood as one, and Marion followed suit. The group sang the first arpeggio, ma-ma-ma-ma-ma-ma-ma, and Patrick glanced at Marion and gave a slight nod. As though to say, come in, you're welcome here. As though to say, today, the man whose life you've shared for the past ten years spoke to you with obstinacy in his voice, and that fierceness told you he's tumbling down a steep, slippery slope, his every word proof that he is not doing well, not at all, and this time you weren't able to step into the breach, you didn't come up with solutions to quell his doubts and, perhaps even more surprisingly, more serious still, you took off after his confession, came here with us, the carefree Monday-night singers, found refuge here among us rather than staying there with him, and I'm here to tell you, Marion, that that is no accident.

# 7

THE STRUCTURE OF THE SMALL SUGAR SHACK WAS STILL
sound. One of the walls had to be opened up to bring in the
new evaporator, but Sylvain gave Adam a hand and the task
turned out to be enjoyable. Adam was bent on keeping the
original wood, and the boards were now piled up alongside the
shack, ready to be used again.

Where the wall had been, Adam imagined a large sliding
door to allow for deliveries and any transfers of the bulky
machines, which Sylvain acknowledged with a barely percep-
tible nod.

"You're the boss, boss," he invariably said.

Adam wondered whether he was being made fun of and
whether Sylvain's repeated declaration of obedience wasn't his
way of making Adam see how ridiculous it all was: the maple
stand, the sugar shack, the grand plans that took hold of men
like him as they aged and had too much money. And the
notion of being the boss, just as laughable. If there was a boss,
it was first the forest, the climate, then the Quebec Maple
Syrup Producers, and far, very far behind, the producer himself. All of which Sylvain knew, and so, by saying, "You're the

boss, boss," more than anything, he had established that Adam didn't have a clue.

That fear came with a wave of deep sorrow: What kind of man was he turning into? Weren't apathy and mistrust the lot of envious people who were chronically dissatisfied, frustrated, who hadn't had enough strength of character to reach for the star to illuminate their family? His mother, his father, his ex-wife. His daughter, possibly, if he couldn't manage to bring her back onto the path of the optimist.

But him?

Whatever the case, Adam was determined not to let it get him down and eventually always chose to believe that Sylvain was a good man with colourful language who loved this land that had once been his, and was simply trying to earn an honest living without having to bid it farewell.

No one could want to leave this land. To see it all, you had to walk along the winding path that climbed between the trees to the top of the hill where a clearing in the maple stand had given birth to dense, diversified vegetation worthy of a country wedding. Wildflowers, clover, a few apple trees. From there, you had a view of all the neighbouring lands. Several orchards teemed with visitors at this time—harvest time—in stark contrast to the silence that reigned in the sugar maple grove. Here, leaves were turning yellow, only to fall to the permanently muddy ground. Plunging into the woods to check on the condition of the tubing, the scent of autumn got you by the throat.

*Strange*, thought Adam as he continued walking, *how much you can love the smell of things rotting.*

Some of the tubing had holes gnawed by rodents or had been damaged by the tractor, but most would hold up, Sylvain assured him. Personally, he saw no immediate need to replace the evaporator; it still had two or three seasons left in it. Adam had insisted on the energy efficiency and ease of use of the new unit he'd found on the internet and ordered from a manufacturer in Bois-Francs. The new system recycled the vapour to generate the energy required to operate the evaporator, a major technological and environmental breakthrough, at least that's what was written on the product information sheet, which Sylvain considered with a dubious eye.

"I don't know," he'd said, "we've used wood to heat our syrup for centuries—are you sure you want to change that?"

To be honest, more than anything, Adam had been attracted to the shiny, stainless-steel purlins on his brand-new machine, its sturdy, recently welded spouts; something about the blank page it represented seduced him. His land had belonged to others, and he still felt a stranger there—as recently as this morning, he mistook a beech for an elm, and the Sweets had laughed, not maliciously, of course, but they did laugh. It seemed to Adam that the new evaporator gave him a certain edge, and even if the desire was childish, he got secret satisfaction from his purchase.

Now he and the Sweets stared at the evaporator the way his father used to stare at the Ferraris in the car dealer's window when he took his children out on Sundays to let their mother "have her nap"—with religious deference. Admiring yet intimidated. Adam's father would never own a Ferrari, an Alfa Romeo, or a Porsche. At most, his brother-in-law would sometimes let him drive his Trans Am during their summers in the Baskatong region.

At those times, his father would shout, *Adam! Manue! Get on in here!*

His mother would stay put on the veranda with their aunts and uncles seated round an ashtray, and point out that her daughter's name was Emmanuelle, not Manue—a nickname she hated—in fact, she often congratulated herself out loud for having given her son a name that was impossible to shorten— at least nobody would massacre *his* name, she'd say.

Emmanuelle readily adopted the nickname. Given a choice, her mother would have preferred Emma, a more elegant diminutive, but Manue had been Manue ever since her first dirt-spattered coveralls. Since then, they'd become her uniform in the garden nursery she worked at in Abitibi, far from their mother and their father's grave, far from Adam and Marion, only close to Lada, her Bernese sheepdog, and Claire, her partner for the past twenty years.

Adam had loved those Sundays spent with his father, admiring the cars in the display windows of the dealers lining the highway, guarded like expensive jewellery at the Bay or like the sculptures cordoned off by velvet ropes in the museum. It was a holy Mass, right down to the incantations his father recited week after week: That one's the same green as my first car, a 1962 Corvair, one I worked all year to buy for myself, boy, did I love that car, I drove all the way to Gaspé with it, we had no money back then, I'd head out with one of my pals and we drove and drove, didn't need anything else, sometimes we slept in the car overnight, other times we were lucky, the weather was warm enough to sleep outside, or folks'd invite us to stay with them, that was before the whole peace-and-love scene so some people were leery, but that didn't matter, we never minded sleeping in my Corvair. After, I met your mother and we needed a normal car, so I sold the Corvair.

Adam and Manue would ask, with a laugh, whether he'd camped out in the car with their mother, too, and their father would give a sly grin and say yes, they had, on Île d'Orléans in late August, early September, and they'd seen the northern lights and it was a magical night.

When they were little, Adam and Manue thought the magic of that special night was connected to the heavenly spectacle. When they were slightly older, they'd shoot each other half-embarrassed, half-curious glances during their father's tale since they'd surmised that his grin revealed something of a sexual nature between their parents, an observation that was both horrifying and fascinating to them. It was only later, with the onset of adolescence, that they saw: that night of the northern lights on Île d'Orléans had been magical because of the many fond promises it held that had never been realized. So they stopped asking.

While Sylvain and Adam finished installing the evaporator, Gerry Sweet went outside to check that the tank's supporting structure was sufficiently solid. He had kept quiet for most of the morning, only nodding when Sylvain asked him a question, not making a sound. He only offered an occasional few words, when necessary, accompanied by a gurgling of mucus or a bronchial crackling. Watching him shake the structure's aging beams, Adam caught sight of the old man's gnarled forearms, surprisingly brawny for a man who seemed so frail. He, too, was a tree.

Near the end, Adam's father's arms had been so thin they'd looked like a child's. During one hospital visit, Adam hadn't recognized him at first. He'd wondered, *Who is that little old lady in my father's room?* His heart stopped for the space of a second because he'd thought, *My father is dead, that's why that woman is here and has taken his place in his bed, my father died overnight.* An intense burning invaded the hollow of his chest, travelled up to his shoulders and down through his arms to his fingertips and even into his skeleton, making him aware of his every mood and move. His impulse was to return to the nurses' station at the end of the hall, but the burning had reached his legs by then, his knees, his feet, one more step and it would have been the end of him, spontaneous combustion smack in the middle of the fourth floor D, palliative care unit, in a hospital in desperate need of renovations.

It took a nursing assistant to snap him out of it, a beaming woman his age who looked ten years older and who, passing by, exclaimed, "If it isn't our Cordon Bleu chef! No wild trout tartar for me today, Monsieur Dumont Jr.?"

Whenever she bumped into him, she teased him about the recipes in *Secrets of DNA*, his first book, a bestseller thanks to the ratings for his fledgling show.

"Tell me, really, where do you ever find Salicornia? I can guarantee it doesn't grow in Loblaws!"

Unleashing another booming laugh, she said, "I'm teasing, just teasing, Monsieur Cordon Bleu! In any case, your father is very proud of you."

That day of the wild trout joke, Adam stared at her, speechless, unable to come up with an answer.

"Hey now, don't go lookin' like that. Your father had a bad night, but he's still got those big movie-star eyes and, as long as he does, works for me, what say you, Monsieur Dumont?"

Adam understood then that the assistant was no longer speaking to him, she was inside the room already and, smiling from ear to ear, had taken the old lady's frail hands between her own.

"Pierce Brosnan. Your father looks like Pierce Brosnan."

Adam had regained the use of his legs and drew closer. His gaze lingered on the childlike hands and arms of the old woman and, coming to the face, he discovered his father, who had turned in his direction and was looking at him with his big movie-star eyes. His relief on seeing the proof was tinged with confusion and embarrassment at having mistaken his father for some unknown woman, and Adam stammered out a trite "Hear that, Papa? She says you look like James Bond. Imagine what she'd say if she'd known you when you were twenty!"

Later, he'd called Manue to relate the episode, and she said, "He's shedding his exterior."

In his head, Adam pictured a dandelion in springtime, the kind you blow on and it flies off in fluffs of grey.

"Are you okay, boss?" Sylvain asked, and Adam blinked as though he'd just woken from a long, convoluted dream.

Sylvain watched his father through the window. "The structure for the tank is sound," he added after a pause. "But we'll let him repair it, okay?"

Adam noticed an obstruction in his throat, a large lump that would have been visible to the eye up close. When he opened his mouth to say, "Of course, no problem, I get it," every word he uttered hurt.

FÉLIX WAS WAITING FOR HIM AT THE BAR, HIS HAIR cropped close, impeccable, his eyes riveted to his phone. He wore the fitted clothing required of him as a waiter. When DNA opened its doors, Adam insisted the staff wear what they liked. He wanted people to feel as though they were among friends. Often the night would end in group parties, tables of people talking to each other in a joyful ruckus that lent itself to flirting and pledges of friendship.

Now that Joseph, his business partner, looked after managing the restaurants, the ambience was resolutely more refined. The wood-panelled walls and stripped-down tables remained, but Joseph had ensured that several stuffed animals were removed from the four corners of the restaurant; the music no longer played as loudly; and the waiters, sommeliers, and bartenders all dressed in black. Félix didn't seem to mind. He had always liked dressing like a TV host or a Mafioso on holiday. An ironed shirt tucked into his pants, a leather belt, everything perfectly cut.

Catching sight of his father, Félix smiled and got to his feet. Their hug gave Adam a strange impression; he no longer quite recognized this body he had held hundreds of times before. Had Félix gone back to playing hockey? Or maybe he went to the kind of gym with glass windows that Adam walked by sometimes, wondering if he himself would ever dare wear shorts and run on a treadmill facing passersby as they returned home from work or dragged their screaming children along behind them. He'd ask his son later.

"I'm glad to see you," Félix said, revealing straight, shiny teeth, the product of three long years spent wearing braces through his teen years—Marion had referred him to a trusted colleague who did a magnificent job on Félix's profile, now strong where it used to be receding. Félix was always happy to see his father, even though, like his sister, he no longer slept over at the Hudson house, other than after family celebrations when he'd had too much to drink to get back into his car. Not so much for his safety, in fact, as because he didn't want to damage the vehicle he loved so much; the money and time he lavished on paying for and maintaining it were undeniable proof of that fact. It didn't have the panache of the cars Adam's father had admired, but it was a classic Jeep, which never went out of style, and Adam himself admitted that driving it— which Félix let him do from time to time—was a pleasure.

Félix checked that his father was okay with a seat at the bar (yes) and with the Bloody Marys he'd ordered for them (yes again). *He's like a little grown-up*, thought Adam, and just about spoke the words aloud, but refrained. Félix would have been offended by the term *little*, especially since he wasn't— little, that is—he was taller than Adam. It was better to dispense with any sentimental father-son flights of oratory for now; Adam had no intention of seeing tears well up as they'd been wont to do against his will over the past three months whenever he let himself feel something.

In any case, he was doing better. Working on his land brought him a great deal of satisfaction and, after her initial annoyance at the news, Marion was beginning to see the advantages. Last Sunday, they'd taken the ferry together so he could tour her round the sugar maple stand, and Marion saw how much good the place did Adam. No, he could tell, the winds of fortune were turning for him.

"Okay, so what's this about maple syrup?" asked Félix as he stirred his Bloody Mary with a stalk of celery.

The restaurant was full. Waiters were busy bringing out burrata salads and letting customers on business lunches taste the wines. Adam and Félix were interrupted by several acquaintances: Félix's colleagues, Adam's professional contacts. People would recognize the father, who'd introduce his son, and it was all very pleasant.

Between two greetings, Adam described his plan to Félix. The maple operation would be a sort of lab, the ultimate creative playing field upon which he'd control every stage of production: the extraction of maple water, the making of the most delicate of mousses, pralines, and macarons. This was how he'd presented his vision at a meeting with the team from his show, advising them the new venture would mean time away from his work there and he'd no longer be able to participate in pre-shooting testing. The team was understanding and agreed to take on the responsibility for choosing recipes. Michel, his producer of the smiling eyes with the look of a man forever on vacation, thought it offered great potential for television.

"We could follow you on your journey, the audience loves that. Adam in sugar maple country!"

With the excuse of a parking meter to attend to, Adam ran for the washroom to curb the cold sweat he'd broken into. The thought of welcoming a TV crew into his safe place, the maple stand, all these people with their rustling jackets and their ringing cellphones, their jokes and their *ease*, was repulsive to him. A hijacking. Telling Félix about it, that reaction now seemed childish, and should Michel decide to bring it up again, he'd be relaxed and proactive. In fact, he'd give him a call later.

Then Félix spoke of his own plans.

*I forgot to ask about his news.* Adam kicked himself, ashamed that his son had had to take the initiative.

With the self-assurance of an advertising exec pitching a product, Félix explained that, with his friend Eddy, he was developing a promising app. It was a dating site designed with foodies in mind. The more well-known apps were an ocean you could drown in before ever finding someone who, on top of fitting the criteria around physical attraction, also shared your interests. His own plan would promote dates between fans of gastronomical trends, biodynamic frizzantes, and innovative microbreweries and still allow the privilege of making a choice based on photos because, let's be clear, we're not going to kid ourselves that we don't want pretty girls on there.

Félix winked at Adam, who couldn't help but wince. Félix noticed and continued, "You're not our target audience, Papa, and our market studies show it's an inescapable criterion."

He couched his argument a number of different ways until Adam conceded that he was right, it was a shame that dating sites were so shallow, but there was no point in being a hypocrite: everyone wants to see pictures.

His son's shoulders, which had tensed up over the course of their conversation, dropped by several centimetres. As a child,

Félix had always been tense, both before and after hockey, upon waking and upon going to bed, and Adam would give him massages during which his son kept his eyes shut.

Félix didn't like to be proven wrong. "He gets that from you," Sarah would often say, "that damn pride."

It was more than pride. It was almost a way of conjuring away the verdict. If proved beyond the shadow of a doubt that he had been either dishonest or mean, Félix, distraught, would shut himself up in his room, immured in total silence, crushed by shame. Sarah would manage to coax him out by showing him that, even though he may have lied to his teacher or insulted his friend, it wasn't like he had *really* meant to, it had been accidental or he'd been influenced by some other idiot—which was sometimes true—and Félix, his face swollen from crying, would eventually nod, come out of his room, and try to make amends. A letter of apology to his friend. Trying extra-hard on his next spelling test. Paying more attention to his little sister. The hours he spent crying and hiding under the covers were exhausting for the whole family, and, in his early teens, when Félix began to talk back or play down whatever he'd said, bent on transforming the intent till the point was conceded, his opponents gradually gave up on taking him on.

Fortunately, Félix was a good kid. A generous, smiling kid who loved people. Affectionate, upbeat, and much more pleasant to spend time with than his sister. Did it matter that he didn't yet have the maturity to admit to his mistakes?

"Show me how it works," Adam said to convince Félix of his interest.

His son then launched into a complicated explanation of algorithms and analyses of his generation's lifestyle choices, and Adam half listened as he scrolled through the profiles on the phone Félix handed him. Would he sign up for these apps if he were his son's age? There was something relaxing about choosing your next love interest the way you'd choose a kitchen appliance. That being said, he wasn't naive, the transaction must involve its share of humiliation and dashed hopes. The Amélies, Kayas, Jennifers, and Catherines followed one after the other in photos that, for the most part, the young women had taken themselves in ordinary (a bedroom, a trail of clothing in the background) or exotic (a turquoise sea, a palm tree, a ski run) surroundings, and Adam felt a wave of heat wash over him.

*It's out of the question*, he warned himself, *you will not cry here; everything's just fine.*

He stared hard at the faces, trying to focus on what his son was saying.

"If we manage to get a clear idea of our customers' tastes, we can better target the kind of match they're looking for, and in our case, we've got the whole foodie universe to explore. I mean, you don't hook up someone who's passionate about pulled pork mole with a vegan who's addicted to smoothies. Once you know that, you can save a lot of people a lot of time."

Karine, Alexandra, Pascale, Florence, Celia. At the sight of this last name, Adam's finger stopped. It wasn't the same girl, of course. To begin with, this Celia wasn't Black—for the longest time Adam and Marion had maintained *they didn't see the colour of people's skin*, brandishing the claim like a badge of virtue; ever since Adèle had lambasted them, they knew they'd been wrong but had no idea what to say instead, so they said nothing: Why go looking for trouble? The Celia onscreen had posed laughing uproariously, showing a row of Hollywoodian teeth, and Adam had never seen the other Celia laugh. No, all he'd seen was her writhing on the wet sand, her thighs lashed by the hundreds of tiny pebbles the waves ferried back and forth, her hands instinctively clutching her knee bent the wrong way, and pain carved into her features. Then, later, at the hospital. Her mother's hand on her shoulder. Celia's eyes a well, an avalanche, a verdict, her gaze forever etched in his memory. Adam began to struggle for air, his respiratory tract was shutting down, like doors slamming, and he was afraid he'd pass out right there in front of his son in his own restaurant. He should call his doctor, ask him again if he might have damaged his lungs. The last time, exuding patience, Dr. Picard had told him no, Adam had only swallowed water briefly that afternoon and his body had recovered over the following days, it was nothing more than an irritation, and the only possible sequels could be psychological, which was not, of course, nothing, he said again, if you feel yourself losing control, I can prescribe what you need to help you through, there's no shame in it, Adam, if you knew how many of my patients take antidepressants, many business leaders among them, and Adam shook his head and cut the conversation short, saying, no thank you, you misunderstood me, I was just asking out of curiosity, I'm fine, thank you.

Now his heart was racing and nausea had taken hold. He was far from fine. Félix was still talking and Adam tried with all his might to concentrate on the movement of his lips, but it was too late. The buzzing in his ears was all he could hear. There was no point in fighting this new squall, it would only end once he was back in the shack alone and, even then, would only mark a brief lull in the storm.

# 8

SUZANNE GRUMBLED AS SHE ADJUSTED THE HORIZONTAL blinds on the front window, the one by the reception area. She preferred exposed windows, which gave the clinic natural light, appreciable in the rather gloomy environment, and never missed an opportunity to remind Marion of that fact.

"Why don't we paint the walls in the waiting room? A nice coral colour, what do you think? Something soft but cheerful, darn it! Why insist on making clinics beige, a cream colour verging on penicillin yellow or, in moments of daring, sage green? I'm against it, totally against it, Marion, and I'm the one who has to look at the walls more than anyone else round here."

Suzanne had no trouble saying what she really thought. *Take me as I am* was her motto. She'd started working at the clinic well before Marion, had been there longer than Claude, and knew more about the patients, their lives, their illnesses, their bereavements, their moves, and their financial hardships than anyone else in the office. Marion had never once considered getting rid of the secretary. Suzanne's motto applied to her as well, when you thought about it, only the other way round. Marion took people as they were, whether it suited her or not.

So she surprised even herself at the flash of irritation she felt as Suzanne lowered the blind to hide the street from sight. Jessie agreed: it was morbid. Marion had to stop herself from rolling her eyes—another surprising reaction. Had she had too much coffee? Caffeine could make her impatient. She had to acknowledge that her mood swings were on the rise. Ever since their tête-à-tête over lunch, Jessie had consulted Marion on anything and everything to do with her wedding. Which flowers do you like better? A dessert table or a layer cake? A DJ or a band? Should we invite the great-aunts and great-uncles or only aunts and uncles? Each question came with a never-ending account on her part of the advantages of one choice, then of the other. Whenever Jesse prattled on during a patient's treatment, Marion didn't find it too distracting. It masked the noise of the instruments and some patients came up with great recommendations. All right, she had to put up with their unintelligible sentences, their jaw gaping, a suction tube or polisher inside their mouth, and instruments and cotton balls had to be removed so they could speak freely, which made for further delays. But Marion was fine with it since that meant she didn't have to talk about what was going on in her own life.

Except that Jessie would also follow Marion into the staff room, the X-ray room, the exam room, the reception area, the cloakroom, and, once, to the door to the washroom, any time she was assailed by doubts. She often had doubts. Generally speaking, Marion had no trouble smiling and listening; she even managed to tease her assistant—on days when Adam was doing well or the day after a choir rehearsal—and on certain days, Jessie's persistence didn't even register with her. However, this morning was another story.

Behind the window, someone had hung a bike high in a tree. It was painted all in white. Tied round one of the brake handles was a small bouquet of artificial flowers. Yellow and pink, with green plastic leaves. Marion recognized the symbol. As did Suzanne; she had seen another one by her sister's place in Rosemont. But Jessie needed it explained to her, she who, when she arrived, thought it was a decoration put there by the municipality. Was there a cycling tour planned for their street? When Marion explained that the bicycles were hung at the scene of accidents that had claimed a cyclist's life as a way of paying tribute to the victim, Jessie grimaced.

"Is it for that woman from the other day?"

The week before, a truck had turned a corner and mowed down a cyclist who was in the truck's blind spot. It had happened quite early in the morning and the clinic was closed. But the next day's papers shared all kinds of details. The victim, a woman in her forties, was the mother of two children, a seven-year-old girl and a nine-year-old boy. She was on her way to the school where she taught math. Turning right, the truck driver hadn't seen her and it was a shout from a passerby—a man out walking his dog—that alerted the driver, who was now out on stress leave, suffering from shock. During a TV interview, the victim's husband said his wife had been well-loved by everyone at the school and that their children adored her and that, since they first met in Paris in the nineties, she had been his rock. She was the one who convinced him to move to

Quebec—the family was originally from Iran and had been living in Pierrefonds for the past fifteen years or so—"an open-minded society full of opportunities." Shohreh had had to go back to school because her degree wasn't recognized here, but even so she had started from scratch, and her students, sir, I can't tell you all the presents they'd shower her with at Christmas and in June, flowers, perfume, chocolates, and Shohreh, now this is funny, Shohreh didn't like chocolate, it gave her a stomach ache, but she would never have told her pupils that; she accepted the gifts and wrote thank-you notes to their parents and was very touched, you know, but afterward she gave the chocolates to us, to me and the kids, so everyone was happy. No one deserves to die that way and Shohreh even less so. It should have been me, sir, I can say it should have been me.

When Marion arrived at the office on the morning of the accident, a security perimeter had been set up on-site. As well as police cars, the truck was still there, as were the misshapen, almost sculptural, bicycle and the cyclist's bike helmet, pink with yellow flowers. It was decorated with metallic stickers, smiling unicorns, cats, and a winking sun.

A seven-year-old daughter, a nine-year-old son.

And now, a white bicycle perched in front of the clinic's large window off the waiting room, and even though she was deeply moved by the sad story, Suzanne found it all a bit much; hadn't a thought been spared for the tenants on the second floor? They'd have to see that bicycle out there for the rest of their days. They'd played no part in the drama: it was an unspeakable tragedy for the family, but was it really necessary to make such a to-do for the neighbours, traumatizing children, demoralizing employees and clients?

Marion gave a sigh that was louder than she'd meant it to be.

"What?" Suzanne defended herself. "You think I'm being cruel? I'm just saying out loud what everyone else thinks."

Another of her favourite fetishes: *saying out loud what others are thinking.* Jessie raised an eyebrow and her mouth twisted into an ambivalent grimace. She agreed with Suzanne, the bicycle cast a pall over the street, and would it really lead to fewer accidents? It could possibly stay up for a few weeks. But indefinitely? No, that was too much. Except Marion had sighed. Marion was annoyed. Worse yet, she was disappointed in them. It was unbearable. So Jessie decided to take Marion's side by criticizing Suzanne.

"Really, Suzanne, I do think we have to try to show a little compassion. We're still alive."

Pleading an X-ray she had to consult, Marion fled, more furious than dismayed: Jessie would be the death of her with all her fawning.

At day's end, Marion hesitated briefly before starting down the tree-lined lane leading to the house. She didn't know what she hoped to find there. Adam might be in one of his frenzied moods, coming up with detailed plans to improve the maple operation somehow, or with a scheme for marketing its products and, should she have the misfortune of offering a critique or merely showing a lack of enthusiasm, he'd become irritable, turn inward, and refuse to speak to her for the rest of the evening.

Or he'd be lying in their darkened bedroom, sunk in the odour of must and bad breath, a vacant look in his eye. On Marion's arrival, he would slowly turn to her, tears welling up.

"I'm scared, Marion, I'm so scared."

He'd hold his arms out to her like a child as he spoke so she would rush over to hug him tight. The first few times, Marion was distressed by the sight. Her big, strong man so weakened, her TV host, her star who'd occasionally give out autographs, her assertive, even dominant, lover so helpless. It was heartbreaking. But now, that state had become habitual, and Marion's pleas for him to see a therapist, after an initially positive reception, had never been acted on. The next day, he felt better and, bringing her the coffee he'd made or the eggs Benedict he'd prepared or the maple pecan bread pudding he'd baked, all for her, he'd apologize for having been such a pain and assure her it was just a bit of fatigue; the whole sugar maple stand business created a lot of stress, but he planned to start jogging again, pronto, which should help him cope and, really, no, she needn't worry.

After, he forgot about jogging, forgot his promises, and it started all over again.

Confronted with someone who refuses to help himself, compassion eventually dries up. Even Marion's, despite her having pulled out all the stops looking for therapists warmly recommended by her contacts and buying natural supplements to lift Adam's mood. From that point on, returning home, she dreaded the moment he'd hold his arms out to her. At the spectacle, she had to repress a shudder of disgust.

Although she'd never have admitted as much to anyone, it made her want to slap Adam, right on those cheeks bathed in tears. Whenever she saw a man crying on TV, she had to stop herself from hurling insults and screaming that she didn't believe him, stop with the whole sham already and get a grip, it was all so off-putting. Then, in shame, she'd caress Adam and shower him with kisses, and he would say, "Oh, Marion, you're so kind, I don't deserve it, I don't deserve a wife as wonderful as you."

Adam's car wasn't there. Lately, that's the way she liked it. Coming home to an empty house.

Alone, she could practise her part out loud. When Adam was home, she listened instead to what she'd recorded of their rehearsals on her phone and sang to herself so as not to disturb him. Otherwise, she waited till she was in the car. But she'd rather sing out loud in the house where sound carried so beautifully, especially in the living room with its cathedral ceiling and undeniable acoustic quality. In that sparsely furnished and spacious room, Marion's voice reverberated and the walls responded. Marion sang well there, sang the way she dreamed of doing. Whenever she heard herself, she was always disappointed by the frailty of her voice, its lack of power and breath, not always on key.

*No matter*, she'd tell herself, *being part of a choir, it won't be noticeable.*

Then she resumed singing. Patrick had decided the choir would present excerpts from his favourite oratorio by Bach: *St. John Passion*. Marion hadn't known it and, as soon as she left that first rehearsal, she downloaded it to listen to on her walk home. She immediately fell in love with the music and the surprising versatility of the German, a language that could be rough in adversity, smooth in bliss. It was a bit long, but they wouldn't be singing the whole thing, and professional soloists would accompany them—a routine practice, apparently. She had a favourite passage, a lively, bouncing, exalted chorus. She hoped it would be part of the concert.

"Will we be doing number twenty-seven?" she asked the following Monday when she bumped into Patrick in the parking lot on arrival, too shy to risk pronouncing the title.

Patrick's face broke into a broad grin and he began singing in impeccable German the recitative that preceded the chorus. "Of course. I love 'Lasset uns den nicht zerteilen,'" he replied without stumbling over a single syllable. Then in approximate French, *"Tu as un bon goût."*

Marion felt a rush of pride.

Ever since, she'd spent more time on the chorus than on the rest of the score. What she loved most was the counterpoint, finding yourself in the middle of a complicated musical phrase, hearing the altos, the tenors, the bass responding in similar flights of poetry, but independently from you. As the chorus reached the end, all the singers came together. The absolute mastery of chaos, which would ultimately lead to the final harmony, filled Marion with a joy she had trouble describing. The piece was difficult to sing and Patrick had to make the various voices rehearse diligently for it all to work, and they only managed it once. But that one time had had the effect of a drug on Marion. That evening, she ignored Adam's state of mind, straddled him as he watched the news on TV, undid his fly, and took possession of his body, biting his lip and directing the whole operation without a word. She came to a stupendous climax in under two minutes.

That rehearsal had taken place a few weeks ago and, now that she thought of it, Adam hadn't touched her since, other than those awful times when he'd cling to her, sometimes pulling her hair, leaving a trail of tears and drool down her clothing.

There was still an occasional yellow leaf on the trees in their yard while all the others lay in a rust-hued carpet under the shade of the spruce, whose green shimmered in contrast. Soon the woods would be so bare that Marion would be able to see the colours of the cars driving past. The end of fall also opened up the view behind the house onto the Ottawa River.

She dug into her pocket to send a text message to Adam, but once she had her phone in hand, she did nothing. The charger was in the kitchen outlet next to the coffee maker, and Marion plugged in her phone.

*He'll give a sign of life at some point*, she thought, and her own indifference made her smile.

How had it come to this? Of course, that collision off the beach had triggered something in him, but Marion refused to believe he could have been that affected by what had clearly been an alarming incident, yet a reversible one, a not overly serious collision—in any case, not for him. If he should ever come across that girl Celia today, wouldn't Adam be ashamed of behaving like some shell-shocked war victim when she was the one who'd been struck by misfortune?

Marion turned her computer on and sat at the dining room table in front of the French windows. The sun was setting.

Darkness descended in one fell swoop in November. Everyone knew as much and yet everyone forgot, the fear of gloomy afternoons like the fear of having a stranger follow you down the street. She should have started supper, but she wasn't hungry. She typed CELIA into her search engine, then let her fingers hover over the keyboard as she tried to remember the girl's last name.

# 9

ADAM WAS IN CHARGE OF THE PASTRY; MARIE THE FILLING. Nathalie looked after the finishing touches and Line did the dishes since, according to her sisters, her cooking skills were so poor she could ruin a scrambled egg.

"We don't often let men in here," Nathalie said, looking up from the recipe book on the counter, her drugstore glasses perched on the end of her nose.

Her gaze, as blue as her brother's and her father's, was both stern and benevolent, an amalgam of attitudes that Adam liked and tried to provoke. He suspected that the Sweet sisters had accepted his participation in that day's Christmas pie-making so that they could serve the pies to their relatives and announce they'd been prepared with assistance from the host of *Adam à table*, known to all, at least to the retirees among them because the others, for the most part, had jobs that limited their screen time. Marie had pointed that fact out as though to apologize for not having heard of Adam's show. By way of apology, but also to tease him—her remark held a hint of amusement and a dismayed fascination with the apparent frivolity of Adam's occupations.

"Life is hard, isn't it, Adam," she retorted any time he had the misfortune of complaining about the pimples the makeup base they used on set gave him or about the boring cocktail parties he'd had to attend with the station's higher-ups.

Benevolence, sternness. What joy they gave him!

"Whose job was it to roll out the dough before me?" Adam asked as he tackled his sixteenth crust.

The kitchen belonging to the Sweets' eldest, Nathalie, was spacious; her husband, a construction entrepreneur, was forever adding on to and *upgrading* it, as he called it. That explained the room's unusual shape, a slightly off-centre cross, and the building materials that differed from one spot to the next. Here a granite counter, there a wooden island; the floor by the sink was made of ceramic tile, the one in the breakfast nook of hardwood. Adam would find the fridge in the *west wing* of the kitchen and the pantry in the *south wing*, Line pointed out ironically as she ushered him into the *palace*. To Adam's eye, Nathalie's kitchen was fairly normal in size; however, he refrained from saying so, knowing they would take his comment for what it was: another confession of wealth. As much as they enjoyed making fun of Adam, Sylvain's sisters did not appreciate any negative judgment being passed on their family, and Adam was careful to criticize nothing. Not intentionally at least. He felt at home here in their patched-together kitchen amid the scents of roasted pecan and maple caramel and, if he could have done exactly as he pleased, he'd have stayed there forever, under a magic spell that shrunk him to the size of a salt shaker or a spice jar, and lived on undisturbed.

"I looked after both," Nathalie responded, "rolling the dough and the finishing touches."

"And for the rest of the year, she'd go on and on about how she was the only one who had to do two jobs on pie-making day," Line added.

Marie nodded. "If only so we don't have to listen to that, Adam, I'm glad you're here. But don't bring shame down on us, you hear! Your pastry's too thick."

Adam smiled. How good it felt to not have to think.

"When we were little, Maman did all the baking without any help at all," Line said pointedly.

The three sisters said nothing for a while as they continued to busy themselves round the kitchen. Then Nathalie did a count. "A dozen pies, plus the meat pies, plus the chicken pot pies, the pork hock stew, the cranberry sauce, the fudge, the fruitcakes—four every year: two with rum and two with syrup. She had to start first thing in November to get it all done. The freezer was so full we had to store some at the neighbours', remember?"

Marie whistled through her teeth with annoyance and said, "That bastard Guindon. He always managed to wheedle himself two or three meat pies in exchange for his services, like we didn't already let him park his tractor on our land."

"The Guindons were always the kind to take advantage," agreed Line, and no one contradicted her.

Other than their eye colour, the three sisters were quite different, at least as far as appearances were concerned. Nathalie was tall and sturdy; her long hair, with its red and blond highlights, fell across her generous bosom, getting caught up in her necklaces of fat, multicoloured beads. She said her pupils—she'd taught Grade 1 for thirty-two years—loved her colourful collection of jewellery because it made her look as though she'd sprung out of the pages of a book to be their teacher. Marie had cropped, non-dyed salt-and-pepper hair. Her emaciated arms betrayed a nervous disposition and the greyish tinge to her skin spoke of heavy tobacco use. Her sisters grumbled whenever she threw her coat over her frail shoulders to go have a smoke outside. Line looked much younger than the other two. Her shapeless outdoorsy clothing, devoid of vanity, made her look like a perpetual student, and her downy hair pulled back in a ponytail accentuated the look. Behind thick glasses, her small eyes were always moist. Adam realized he no longer remembered the colour of his own sister's eyes. He closed his own and called up Manue's face. He could see a rebellious cowlick. And her amused, distant expression. But impossible to remember the colour of the irises of her eyes. Would he eventually know these three strangers better than his own family?

Adam dropped the dough he'd been shaping to observe them: Nathalie using her index finger to crimp the crust of a pie ready for the freezer, Marie with her nose in the steam from the boiling sugar, and Line with her yellow-rubber-gloved hands plunged in boiling dishwater. A gush of warm liquid ran through Adam's veins, reaching every part of his body. The sensation was that of a drug taking effect after hours of pain, when you understand with immense relief that there is an end to the suffering and that your time to die has yet to come. In this poorly appointed kitchen, equipped with light fixtures bought on sale in the hardware section of big-box stores and decorated with reproductions of generic rural scenes, among these three women, Adam felt the purest possible bonds.

The bonds of family, yet it was more than that. It was love, and love found its strength in multiple guises, which Adam knew, and he was never without. Marion loved him and he loved Marion. He felt no desire for the Sweet sisters, at least not in the usual sense. He had no wish to sleep with them. He wanted to be near them. In their presence, he grew calm, a participant. That was it—these women, and with them their brother and their father, had the power to give his life back to him, and the minute he distanced himself from them, everything grew cold and suffocating all over again. In their company, Adam tasted the sweetness of life. Oh! How good it would be to bring Marion here, Félix and Adèle, too, how wonderful it would be to immerse themselves together in that reassuring calm; that's when they'd see he had come back to life and they'd stop worrying, and he would share with them the secret to happiness, found in a pie and in the simplest of tasks.

"You've got to start rolling your dough or it'll be too warm, big guy," said Nathalie, who was waiting for him to finish so she could continue.

Adam immediately tackled the smooth ball of dough. As Nathalie had predicted, the dough was warm. It rolled out easily, supple and elastic. Most likely it would not be as flaky once baked. And it stuck slightly to the rolling pin. Soon Marie would tell him to sprinkle more flour on the counter, and Line would accuse him of falling asleep on the job.

Adam would revel in their rebukes.

# 10

FÉLIX CLAIMED THAT THE TIME FOR FACEBOOK HAD COME and gone, that only old fogies and activists still used it, and that you had to wade through the swamp of spiteful or trivial comments before finding anything of interest.

People his age, he said, were found on Instagram.

Well, if Celia had signed up for Instagram, it must be under a pseudonym because Marion hadn't found her there. She did show up on Facebook, and Marion managed to find out that three years earlier, she had gone on a school trip to Washington, where she posed in front of the statue of Abraham Lincoln. Next came a few group photos taken in restaurants that had been posted by members of her family—in fact, almost nothing on Celia's page had been posted by her.

For no particular reason, Marion went back to the page a few hours before the choir's Christmas concert. She should have been drinking herbal tea to soothe her throat and using the flat-iron to look presentable, but there she sat at the kitchen table in front of the computer as evening fell. Adam wasn't home—he'd meet up with her at the church, he said in his text message; he was held up with some task or other at the Sweets'.

She didn't find anything much that was new. Two or three pictures and a video of the small saltwater taffy factory where Celia worked. The workshop doubled as a shop: customers could choose among over forty flavours of soft taffy. Lemon, caramel, strawberry, mint, licorice, grape. The video showed how the taffy was made using a machine with large hooks that stretched the rope, and Celia's hands and arms could be seen inserting it into some sort of gear—the equipment looked to be straight out of another era—from which emerged machine-wrapped candies in wax paper.

Marion had to watch the video twice to be sure it really was her since her face could only be seen for a few seconds and her hair was hidden beneath a white hairnet. She looked so young. But Celia was, in fact, young, wasn't she? She had the open gaze of a child; her face shadowed by huge bags under her eyes, and her oversize T-shirt sporting the logo of the taffy shop made her look like an orphan, one who was trundled here and there, her only clothing ill-fitting odds and ends that had been scrounged from a lost-and-found bin.

Captions with catchy phrases were designed to attract tourists to Martha's Vineyard for a taste of the authentic east coast. So, this was how Celia spent her days before the tragedy? Had she hoped to take over the family business and, after much hard work and many a setback, open a branch and make her ancestors proud?

Except that, since July, she'd written nothing on social media. Only one comment in response to a girlfriend's post on her page, something cryptic and innocuous about a kitsch reality show the two seemed to find amusing. The comment, written a few weeks earlier, was proof that Celia was still alive and able to write, two things Marion found reassuring. But the girl's inactivity bothered her. Alive and able to write did not mean she might not be in a pitiful state. Maybe she was bedridden, in a wheelchair, paralyzed by chronic shooting pain that left her haggard and depressed. Maybe she'd lost her boyfriend, too much of a coward to look after a young woman who'd been disabled. Not to mention the barbarity of the U.S. health system, and Celia was not well-to-do; everything pointed to that fact—her clothes, the places she hung out, no, she probably had very little insurance coverage and had to work herself ragged to pay for her treatment. Not to mention the trips to the hospital, calculating the cost of gas and compensating for her disability at work. Under those kinds of conditions, who would feel carefree enough to write rubbish on a dying social network, as though life still went on? Marion shuddered and turned off the computer.

She glanced at the clock on the stove. Five-forty. She'd have to eat something soon to avoid singing on an empty stomach and feeling dizzy. Going onstage right after too heavy a meal was no better and could cause even more embarrassment. Soup and a bit of bread. She would finish the squash soup Adam had brought home the day before. One of the Sweet sisters had insisted he give it to Marion. Stirring the soup on the stovetop with her wooden spoon, she told herself she still hadn't met these women Adam had grown so close to over the past few weeks. Any curiosity she might feel about them, there was no denying it, was non-existent. Yet she was annoyed.

Was it the weird, good-natured tone in Adam's voice whenever he spoke of them that made her jealous?

Was she jealous?

Marion didn't think so. She was happy to know someone was looking after him and, to tell the truth, he'd been much easier to get along with since he'd started spending time with them. They must embody some kind of familial substitute for Adam, poor little lost boy.

*Poor little lost boy.*

Marion stopped stirring, amazed at the ease with which she had formulated the unkind thought. She understood—or was it more of a hunch since, although she derived an odd measure of pride from dispensing with niceness, she would never have said anything of the sort in Adam's presence; it was one thing to think it, quite another to say it out loud—that she was undergoing a change. It was impossible to know whether hers was due to Adam's own transformation since the accident; however, she couldn't help noticing that, far from seeking to blame the young girl on the beach through whose auspices the crisis had occurred, she harboured anger toward him, his weakness, his selfishness, his lack of resilience. Whenever she let the contempt in, it flooded through her like a raging stream and she was stunned by the thought, so on the mark, so pitiless, she had formulated so effortlessly.

As though she'd been preparing for this moment from the start.

AFTER THE CONCERT, SHE FELT A BRIEF PANG WHEN ADAM appeared in the small vestry behind the altar that served as backstage for the choir members. He searched her out, his gaze misted over, an elegant bouquet of flowers in his hand. He seemed lost suddenly, stripped of his fame and the cushion of relationships that gave him permission to plow through any crowd as though above it all. Here, in the anglophone milieu of a choir from the outskirts of Montreal, his name and his face were unknown. He was Marion's fella, and the other singers' curiosity went no further than that.

He seemed shaken. Whether by the concert or by the sight of Marion onstage, it was too early yet to say. Touched, Marion hurried over to him.

"It was magnificent, you were magnificent," he said.

Everything had moved him, the obvious joy of the choir, the beauty of the musical selection, the church's acoustics. His eyes were still damp, as though he stood forever on the threshold of the house of tears, unable to decide whether to enter, yet not leaving the premises either. When Marion took his hand to lead him toward Patrick and the others, he was shaking.

Patrick greeted him warmly, and Marion was surprised to realize his handshake was stronger than her partner's. Adam's forearm was pulled low by Patrick's grip. Some ten centimetres shorter than Adam, Patrick glowed, and beside him, the others seemed paler under the neon lights.

"*Tu avais aimé ton soirée?*" Patrick asked, truly interested in the answer.

Marion noticed just how charmed she was by Anglophones mistakenly using the familiar *tu*. From a Francophone, it would have been forced familiarity. Not that it bothered her all that much, several of her patients used *tu* with her from the very first appointment on and she didn't hold it against them. But when it was the result of an unfamiliarity with the language, she found it irresistible, alive.

*"J'ai beaucoup aimé ma soirée,"* said Adam.

Had he stressed the *ma* to signal to Patrick his mistaken use of *ton*? Adam had been so subdued tonight, as though someone had wrapped him in a blanket, the kind you use to soothe a dog made nervous by thunderstorms. It would have been surprising for him to try to deliberately humiliate Patrick. Despite which, Marion hoped he wouldn't tag along to the pub, where the choir planned to celebrate the end of the fall term.

Once all the congratulations had been extended and received, Marion and Adam made their way toward the exit.

"The others are going for a bite at the pub," Marion said. "Did you want to come?"

Adam glanced at his watch and sighed. He wasn't annoyed. It was a sigh of lassitude so loaded with meaning that Marion just about burst into tears. And yet, when he said he was exhausted and had been in the studio filming all morning before visiting the Sweets, that he'd come straight to the concert without showering, and that if she didn't mind too terribly, he'd like to bow out and go home to bed, Marion's heart swelled with almost euphoric relief. In gratitude, she hugged him close, the warmth of her cheek glued to the stubbled cheek of her beloved.

"Go rest, my love. I won't be too long."

Some drove to the pub, but Marion decided to walk. As did Patrick. The winter air was brisk and sweet-smelling and she didn't regret her choice. Later, after her throat had been scraped raw from all the laughter and talking over each other in the crowded pub, and when it was time to leave and go for their cars, they hadn't realized that the temperature had dropped. The liquor kept them warm. The liquor and the joy that came from budding friendships.

Marion explained to Patrick her love for British TV series set in Northern England—Yorkshire, for example, where he told her his ancestors used to live before crossing the ocean 115 years earlier.

"When they mention a family member," she explained, her breath turning to ice, "they always say 'our' before his or her name. *Our* Alison, *our* Henry, *our* Edna. As a constant reminder of the bond tying them to others, not just the personal bond, but their bond as a group. I think I'm moved by people who think in terms of *us*."

Patrick listened with a smile. He hated to disappoint her, but no one ever spoke that way in his family of ordinary *maudits Anglais*. Marion felt a sharp twinge of disappointment when they reached the church parking lot. Their cars were the only two left, blanketed in a light sprinkling of sparkling snow. Marion thought of Adam lying in their big, comfortable bed, moonlight dividing the room on the diagonal since he wouldn't have closed the curtains all the way.

"Would you like one last drink?"

Marion nodded.

She followed him in her car to his apartment in a relatively new and rather ordinary condo building near the outskirts of Hudson.

Patrick went ahead of her and grabbed a pile of clothes off the floor. He threw them into a closet as he pointed out that hiding his mess in front of her defeated the whole purpose, and Marion didn't wait another second before planting a kiss on his lips right then and there, between the closet and the bathroom door.

He kissed her back without hesitation and, once they were done, she took a step back to look at him.

She'd felt her desire growing over the course of the evening; it was the way he conducted the singers, received the accolades and returned the compliments, and, above all, the way he looked at her when she spoke—not with blind admiration, no. It wasn't that he wanted her either, *wanted to get his hands on her*, in bed or elsewhere. He simply seemed to rejoice in the fact that she existed. That type of no-strings-attached attention was totally foreign to her. And irresistible.

"Are you going to kiss me again?"

Later, when she'd think back to that evening, she wouldn't remember which of them asked the question. But it didn't affect what was to follow because they kissed for hours, and when she put her clothes back on to go home, daylight had started to filter through the window of her choirmaster's bedroom.

# 11

SARAH SAID, "I GIVE UP."

Sarah said, "It's your turn now, what's more, all that glorifying of atypical paths, that's your doing. You're the one who's always told them how you yourself are 'self-made,' how school bored you sick and how you said to hell with it, you're the one who not only dropped out of business admin to take up cooking because you'd supposedly found your passion, yet you didn't even bother finishing your pastry training because 'the instructors had no instinct for it' and you weren't learning a thing. You're the one who boasted every time you gave up on commitments: quitting right in the middle of a shift because the chef was a 'dictator' or the customers had 'a broomstick up their ass'—not dwelling on the mess you left behind for your colleagues, who all had to do double duty just to make it through the rest of the evening—from there to your aborted plans for a restaurant, a catering service, a fast-food outlet, a food truck before they were a thing, all the hilarious, sexy stories of your woes, trials, each financial abyss, the squabbles and destroyed friendships, you've told them since they were kids as though recounting the adventures of a hero destined for great things, barely mentioning—what do I mean *barely, never* is more like it—the role I had to take on over all those years, the deadly boring jobs I had to put up with, unable to quit because the rent and the kids' boots needed to be paid for, and worst of all is that, of course, those great things did come to be, success found you, and with it the branches and media offers and spinoff products even as, oh, so sad, such a shame, your first marriage was ending because we 'had taken different paths.' Actually, of the two of us, you were the only one who had a choice as to which path to take, and because of you, today the kids see me as an incarnation of all that is overly cautious and dull, an unremarkable, unattractive being who didn't take enough risks in life, when just living with you all those years was its own goddamn risk, Adam, but I can't tell them that, I'm a good mother, I don't speak ill of my ex to my children, I keep it for my girlfriends during our Friday-night dinners washed down with plenty of wine but lacking in tales of sexual exploits since fewer and fewer men are interested in us, we're too pissed off, and pissed off is a turnoff; hey, use that on a T-shirt, you'll make another fortune. It's your turn now, Adam, I'm done."

Adam had never seen her so furious. It gave her the bright red cheeks of a child back from playing in the snow. He found her beautiful and almost said so. But she wasn't through.

"I gave everything I had—my energy, my goodwill; I gave of my time, so much time, if you only knew, and you don't know—don't go thinking you have the faintest idea of what it means to be responsible for the well-being, the safety, the survival, the development of two human beings—and I can hear you muttering under your breath that I wouldn't be as tired if

I wasn't so hard to please, that if I'd let you do things *your way*, we wouldn't have reached this point, let me shut you down right there, Adam, because I never stopped you from doing a single thing, I didn't even stop you from getting the fuck out, and there's no way you can come crying to me with that now, not today. Your daughter decided that college is pointless and that she's smarter than her profs, her mother, and the whole of society. How am I supposed to contradict her? What do I know, anyway? I'm an idiot, Adam, that's the conclusion your daughter has come to about me, and, frankly, when I look at how I let everyone treat me like a pile of shit over the past twenty years, I can do nothing but agree. And, of course, a pile of shit cannot guide a genius; however, this pile of shit can decide she's had it up to here and surrender to you the keys to Adèle's destiny so you can bring your magic touch into play, the way you do with your restaurants, your shows, and your girlfriend's breast implants, so I wish you good luck, Adam, and I myself will put our dear daughter's clothes into the trunk of your car because it's over."

Sarah sat on a chair in the kitchen, the kitchen in which they used to prepare baby food for their children, made love once, and decided to separate. In the meantime, she had changed the colour on the walls, but the floor tiles, the all-purpose kind of subway tile, hadn't changed; the night he told her he no longer loved her he'd followed the lines of grout with his gaze.

She wasn't crying, but that was worse. Was this the right time to tell her he wasn't really doing well, that the only places he felt happy were in his sugar maple stand and the kitchen of a fiftysomething woman from the North Shore? That he couldn't imagine a worse role model for his daughter than a man paralyzed by grief and that there was a strong likelihood he would opt to pay for her to have an apartment instead of letting her stay with him too long since Adèle's presence reminded him of what he had been unable to pass down to her, and it was already hard enough having to see his own reflection in the mirror without entertaining those other thoughts.

Yet "Marion doesn't have breast implants" was the one and only thing he said before he grabbed the cardboard box with his daughter's cosmetics and winter boots inside, and slid it onto the back seat of his car.

ADÈLE WAS FUMING MAD. HOW COULD HER MOTHER HAVE delivered such a slap in the face? Abandoning her without an ounce of compassion for the ordeal—the crisis—she was going through? Now she doubted every value her mother had ever pretended to tout. Sarah had promised never to impose a thing on Adèle, that she would always be free to be herself, that she was *perfect just as she was.* Ha! What a lie that was: now that her daughter had veered off the conformists' path of studies you cruise through, leading to a pathetic job in the service of a corrupt system, that same sweet mother had thrown her out, obstructing the courageous path she was on. She was forcing her to move half a world away, to suburbia, when she knew full well that such a change would be anxiety-provoking and prej-udice her chances of *finding herself.* Never had she thrown Félix out, despite his failing French lit in college and never getting his degree! Okay, Félix moved out of his own free will into an apartment, but what kind of message was she being given here? Exploit like her brother the gullibility of rich people ready to give you hundred-dollar tips in a bourgeois restaurant while acting like the worst possible douchebag, dress up as a rich girl, and you'll see, money will rain down on you? No thank you, Adèle had real values, and the moral prostitution that ran rampant in such trendy venues stank. She should point out that she had nothing against sex workers and, in fact, maybe that's the profession she should choose, let's see what her mother would think then.

Adam watched her hang her clothes up in the closet in the guest bedroom, dump her cosmetics onto the bathroom counter, then slam all the kitchen cupboard doors, trying to unearth a box of cereal or a bag of cookies, you never have anything to eat, your girlfriend's for sure anorexic, did you know that? And he thought of what Nathalie and Marie had told him, just after Sarah's phone call summoning him to pick up Adèle's things.

"If you want your kids to respect you," Marie told him, "start by showing them you see through their bullshit."

Nathalie added, "No one feels loved if they're being ignored."

"I don't ignore her," Adam said in his defence. "In fact, it feels like I spend my whole life giving in to her whims."

"To begin with, you've been looking after your kids on a very part-time basis, if that, for the past ten years. That takes away your right to say you *spend your whole life* doing anything for them," Nathalie stated.

"Get it? We see through your bullshit. And we're telling you so because we care," concluded Marie.

Adam felt the same warmth that enveloped him every time a member of the Sweet family showed any sign of affection, and he took a couple of seconds to savour it. The rest was quick to follow.

"Second," Nathalie decreed, "not ignoring your daughter does not in any way mean giving in to her every whim. It means hearing what she has to say, and, above all, asking yourself why she's saying it. What does your daughter need? Love, for sure, but that she got from her mother and from you, even though she must certainly have felt less important than your girlfriend or your work. The truth, maybe. Your daughter needs the truth. Are you capable of giving her that?"

Adèle poured some Cheerios into a coffee cup, then drowned them in milk.

"Hey, quit staring at me," she said, annoyed.

Adam thought: *Why did she choose a cup instead of a bowl? Was it her taking a stance? Was it to come across as original? If I ask her, will she take it the wrong way, storm out of the kitchen, and slam her bedroom door?* Adam knew he was too fragile to cope with any of that, the slamming of the door, the tension, the hours-long silence, and all of a sudden he felt great distress and regretted Marion's absence. No doubt she would have known what to do, what to say.

"That's the other problem," Marie added. "By saying nothing, you let your girlfriend shoulder the whole burden. It's a heavy load for her, and it's debilitating for you."

She might not have said "debilitating." She might have said *it leaves you powerless.* Wasn't it more or less the same thing? The absence of power, paralysis. Nathalie and Marie thought he owed his daughter the truth. But which truth? That she was insufferable and he fully understood why no boy took an interest in her with that permanent scowl on her face and her annoying little eccentricities? That today he'd had a humiliating meeting with his producer, during which Michel had squirmed in his chair, embarrassed at having to tell him that the broadcaster had received complaints about his rambling hosting style—the video clips he'd shown didn't lie—and what would he think of extending his vacation after the holidays? His colleague from the Italian cooking show, Rita, could help them out; her popularity was growing and she had managed to attract millennials to her show thanks to her funny, dynamic presence on social media. That he'd started dreaming about his own mother again and that, in his dreams, she reamed him out for not looking after her, rattling off his mistakes, starting with that time he hadn't been able to hold it in on his way home on the school bus, and the principal had told her, "Madame, if you use mayonnaise on your son's sandwiches, you'll have to keep them cold, especially in June"? She'd made him wash his underwear himself. In the dream and in real life, too. Had he ever told Adèle that story? Had he ever told anyone?

"Adèle, be gentle with me. Please."

His daughter stopped chewing to stare at him. It was as though the air between the two of them had quit circulating. Had he tried to draw a breath, Adam would probably have discovered there was no oxygen left in the room. He waited, and it felt like the objects in the kitchen waited, too, on guard and terrified, for her to say something. A memory came to him of an animated film she used to like as a child where all the objects spoke to each other: a clock, a teapot, a candelabra. What was the title of that movie? She must have watched it a hundred times and he'd forgotten to remember the title. If whether a child was gentle with her parent was the reflection of the salary for that parent's competency, then he didn't deserve his wage. But he'd asked for it all the same. With hope.

"Okay," Adèle replied.

She lowered her gaze to the spoon poised halfway between the cup and her mouth, as though the spoon were wondering what it was doing there in this kitchen witnessing heartache between a father and his daughter. What had Adèle heard in her father's voice that made her lose her fury? Had she felt pity for him—or had she seen in him her own reflection?

Adam was overcome with the desire to ask her to forgive him, to ignore what he'd just said. He was a pathetic moron and she had nothing at all in common with him. But he didn't.

Adèle put her cup in the sink, rinsed it, asked whether the dishes in the dishwasher were dirty or clean. Adam managed to say they were dirty, so Adèle put her cup and spoon inside. Then she emptied the sink strainer into the garbage because all the Cheerios had glommed together there. She put the cereal box back in the cupboard.

She didn't say another word.

# 12

MARION HAD NEVER SEEN HERSELF IN THE ROLE OF THE unfaithful woman, and she was curious to discover what sort of unfaithful woman she was proving to be.

Whenever someone brought up the issue of adultery, at the end of a dinner, for instance, when one of her male friends—in an advanced stage of alcohol consumption, thinking it was a good time to stir up a bit of shit—put it out there that it was impossible for a normally constituted human being to remain faithful to just one person for the rest of their life, Marion invariably said, "I'm so loyal, I'd have to be head over heels in love for it to happen to me."

And no one questioned her statement, contrary to those made by other guests whose convoluted attempts at justification gave rise to many a knowing glance and unspoken judgment. All were in agreement, though, where Marion was concerned. She was, in fact, *so loyal.*

Adam smiled and draped his arm round his sweetheart's shoulder, declaring that was the reason he'd chosen her, for her loyalty, her reliability, a truly good little woman.

He said it for a laugh, of course, knowing the qualifiers were not to Marion's liking and that, even if they did describe her, that was not why he loved her. Marion too laughed. What bound her to Adam was much deeper—and inexpressible. Some unknown factor, the genuine suffering at the thought of their being separated. Despite Adam's proud and naively seductive side, Marion had never worried about him sleeping with other women.

"I'd have to be head over heels in love for it to happen to me," she'd said.

And yet, there she was, lying naked in another man's bed, absent-mindedly stroking her eyebrows as he had a shower, and she saw with staggering acuity that she was neither in love with him nor on the way to being so.

They saw one another two more times after the concert, that waking dream from which she emerged feeling light and invigorated. Back home, there was no need for explanations. Adam was fast asleep, which hadn't happened for a long time, and she was able to linger in the shower, slip into her pyjamas, and stretch out on the couch, wrapped in the plaid blanket off the reading armchair. When he woke, she was laughing and incandescent, blaming the alcohol and the fries for a night spent on the couch digesting both, and Adam told her again how marvellous she'd been at the concert and what a great group they seemed to be.

She smiled. "They are, they're wonderful."

*How easy it is*, she'd thought.

The second time was out of curiosity. Patrick had sent her a sweet, laconic message the next afternoon, something like *hope you're okay, not too tired*, accompanied by an emoji crying with laughter to lighten the tone, a neutral message that, had it been intercepted by Adam, would not have given rise to suspicion.

Marion quickly replied, *more than okay, feeling great*, and it was true.

She watched the dancing dots appear, disappear, and reappear on her screen, and felt her chest constrict: Patrick was nervous. Hesitant. Did he regret their night together?

She didn't wait any longer to type *are you okay?* But their messages crossed paths and she received his lengthy reply before he'd read her question. No matter, since he answered it.

What he said was, more or less, I don't want to cause problems for you, someone once interfered with the relationship I had with a woman and it only made matters worse. I don't want to make anything worse for you. I want to make everything easier for you, more light and airy.

*Make it light*, he'd written in English. A word meaning both lightness of being and a source of light, and it was lovely, thought Marion.

She replied: *when can I see you again?*

And he: *asap.*

The acronym lessened somewhat the charm of the conversation, but Marion didn't hesitate: *thursday.* Adam would be filming a holiday special late into the evening in front of a live audience. *I'm managing my infidelity like a pro*, she noted with surprise.

That being said, there were fewer and fewer things that surprised her.

Their meeting had been strange; after that first night spent in urgent exploration of their new-to-the-other bodies, they had had to face one another sober, without costumes or the sheen of drunkenness.

That first night, Marion hadn't noticed the melamine kitchen and the serving hatch that opened onto the dining room, or the sadly formal aspect of that room with its furniture in dark contoured wood.

"A poisoned inheritance," Patrick said with a laugh, but his laughter revealed his nerves, producing a certain lassitude in Marion. That was not what she wanted.

Later, by the fridge, he'd grabbed her, and she thought, *Oh, here it is, that remarkable strength beneath the flaking skin, the irresistible enthusiasm, uh-huh, really, that's what I want.* She didn't regret that time either.

Now she wondered if the escapade hadn't surreptitiously begun to turn into something resembling a relationship should she want one.

He'd written *want you now* while Marion, making her way home, found herself in a traffic jam on Highway 40.

She smiled at the dramatic pull of the message and reread it before deleting it. She deleted them all as soon as she received them. She might be an adulterer, but she wasn't cruel, and although she didn't know why she was acting this way or how long the affair would last, she did know without the shadow of a doubt that it wasn't to punish Adam and that she had no desire to hurt him.

She didn't text back for the duration of Joni Mitchell's album *Blue*—the traffic was a good buffer between a first impulse and reasoned action—then, once she was on Hudson's main street, she turned left at the intersection and drove to Patrick's without telling him.

Now she sat listening to him sing an air from a baroque opera in the shower. It was still light out. If someone happened to pass in front of Patrick's condo building, they could have recognized her car in the parking lot. Adam could see it, or even Adèle, should she decide on the spur of the moment to go for a walk, which, truth be told, would never happen. Since her arrival, her stepdaughter did nothing but ask for lifts downtown or retreat to her room, where she sat on the bed, her eyes glued to the screen of her laptop.

Sometimes Marion asked what she was doing, using the most neutral tone of voice she could muster, and Adèle would shrug, then say, "Stuff."

She was doing stuff.

"Cool," said Marion before walking on.

Often, Adèle would ask her to close the door behind her, and Marion felt as though she were her employee. She wondered if it was the lack of a genuine bond between Adèle and her that made it seem that way or if Sarah got the same feeling.

How had she ended up here, six months shy of her fortieth birthday, lounging on her lover's bed one Wednesday afternoon just before Christmas when she should have been busy buying last-minute presents for the many children everyone, and especially her, had thought she would have by this time?

*Marion's a little mother*, her father would always say to get a rise out of Myriam when they were little.

He didn't grasp the fact that the statement, on the contrary, rid her sister of all kinds of pressure.

"They've been expecting me to disappoint them from the day I was born," Myriam told her one day, laughing. "Why deprive them?"

For Marion, things were different. They had predicted nothing but success. Of course, step-grandchildren were not real grandchildren, not when you first met them when they were already eight and ten and you only saw them once a year.

"It's not a question of loving them," Gisèle kept saying, "we have love to spare, isn't that right, Raymond, we love those two kids big-time! But we never see them! Bring them over, bring them over!"

Beneath her parents' good nature and relaxed air, there lay, lurking behind their gifts of money for Adèle and Félix and vows that they were a "chosen family," the increasingly aggressive impatience of grandparents who'd been shortchanged. On the surface, everyone played the game, and both Gisèle and Raymond were bound and determined to prove they had a *modern* view of what constituted a family.

Patrick emerged from the bathroom that opened onto his bedroom (another door gave access to guests without having to pass through the bedroom, a detail meant to be clever, a way of offering the much sought-after ensuite in a three-bedroom apartment) and sat down next to Marion. The beads of water on his body fell gently onto Marion's shoulder and Patrick wiped them off with his finger, both embarrassed and fascinated at having left a trace on her.

"You're magnificent," he said in English with a smile, and Marion understood that he was sad—and sincere.

She looked at her own body in the full light of day, trying to see it through his eyes. It had taken her years to let Adam see her in broad daylight and, if she did so nowadays, there was a certain calculated element to the gesture. Unflattering angles were proscribed and she never *walked* naked unless they were in the dark.

Yet here she remained naked with disarming ease in front of a man she barely knew. She had only to reach out to cover herself with the sheet.

Instead, she caressed the red patch on Patrick's neck.

"Does it hurt?"

"Not today."

"Do you want to put on some lotion?"

"Not in front of you."

"What are you doing for Christmas?"

"Family, Winnipeg. And you?"

Marion could see her parents' apartment, Gisèle's turkey, her father's cantaloupe and prosciutto—that he'd been adamant about serving since the turn of the century—Adam's dessert, something maple-based, maybe he'd insist on serving one of the pies from the Sweet family she had yet to meet. Félix would serve up nightclub-worthy cocktails while making plans to go out with his friends later; Adèle would for all intents and purposes remain mute, unless neither of them showed up, and Sarah would have them both the day before Christmas *and* on Christmas, as was her wont, without any sign of protest from Adam.

Patrick laid his palm on Marion's temple. With the tip of his thumb, he began stroking her cheek. It was rough and warm. Not unpleasant.

"I'm going to my sister's in Vancouver," she said out of nowhere.

Hearing the words, she knew that that's what she would do. And that the fling with Patrick was over.

# 13

"I BOUGHT MYSELF A SUGAR MAPLE STAND," ADAM REPEATED, only louder this time.

His producers were known for throwing the most popular parties in the business, and they hadn't disappointed this year. Held in a former factory that had been converted into a contemporary art gallery in Griffintown, the celebration had the air of an after-gala event. Employees, colleagues, and the other satellites of celebrities—in this milieu, those in the shadows were not necessarily the least powerful—all exhibited the euphoria and complacency associated with having attained the markers of success: awards, recognition, money.

The crowd pulsated to such an extent they could have raised the roof to let in the flaky, cinematic snow that was falling that evening. There was magic all the same since the factory's ceiling had been replaced by a huge skylight, revealing the play of projectors that a young multimedia entertainment company had installed on the roof.

"Is there anything other than young multimedia entertainment companies in Montreal?" Adam jeered to one of the show's junior producers, concerned by the bitterness of his tone that was meant to be friendly.

But the producer, who looked to be his son's age, laughed and said there were organic wine bars, too.

Adam thought, *If we can't laugh at ourselves*, and he silently congratulated himself for his composure. It would be a good party: he was already tipsy and nothing scared him.

Now was the time for cocktails and gossip, but the music was already playing loudly, a sign the guests would soon be heading for the dance floor. The young producer made his way to the smoked fish table while trumpeting the evening's commandments: drink fast, eat first, dance lots, and, with a little bit of luck, find someone to kiss in a corner; with a lot of luck, find someone to kiss in a cab on the way to just one address.

Adam raised his glass of champagne as a sign of approval, an absent-minded smile on his lips. Did he remember having led that kind of life at one time? All the drinking, eating, fucking had been there for him—he hadn't lost his memory. Yet now he noticed that it no longer did anything for him. He had just read an article in the newspaper—or was it on the radio? When the report caught his attention, through the window of the sugar shack, Adam had been watching a chipmunk fill its cheeks with tubers before ducking into a hole beneath the building, only to return and start digging again. A trauma specialist was describing a treatment designed to rid people who had suffered a post-traumatic incident of the terror reflex. Under the influence of medication usually meant to regulate cardiac arrythmia, the patients recounted the traumatic event during several sessions over a number of months. The female specialist claimed the results were impressive. People forgot nothing; they knew what they'd been through. Yet they no longer felt distress at what had made them suffer so. They could call up the circumstances of the rape, the assault, the war, without attaching an emotion to it. Adam was reminded of that now, amid silent films from the New Wave—the party had a sixties theme—with the loudspeaker belching Dutronc's *"le monde entier est un cactus."* He thought to himself that that was what had happened to him.

Drinking, eating, fucking.

He had been desensitized.

The memory of his partying years made him feel neither regret nor longing.

"So, when do we go outside and roll bare-chested in the snow?"

The question came from a man who had approached him, and Adam took a minute to make out his features in the dim light.

"Ready when you are," said Adam, giving Nicolas the virile hug of men who like a show of affection but are mindful of their image.

Nicolas Bocci had been one of DNA's most loyal customers when it started and had contributed to Adam's fame by sending to his restaurant a continuous flow of wealthy contacts from the most influential circles—business, politics, entertainment—who loved good food. Over time, the two had become friends—at least, until recently, that's what Adam would have said. If he had bumped into the man while with someone who hadn't met him before, Adam would have introduced him thus, *This is my friend Nico, we've gotten into all kinds of trouble together*, and Nico would have added, *And then some*. Adam would have said, *Good to see you*, and Nicolas would have moaned, *With Adam's being a TV star now, he's never found at his own restaurant anymore, and hey, doesn't he miss all those rounds of grappa with his best customers, the ones who stay late?* They would have laughed and promised to get together soon— Adam might even have floated the suggestion of a barbecue at his house, why not?

But now Adam looked at Nicolas and was puzzled by the lack of emotion he felt in the man's presence. Drinking, eating, fucking, Nicolas Bocci. What else could he add to the list?

"What's new, you rotter?" asked Nicolas, his gaze distracted by a woman with lustrous locks passing by.

"I bought myself a sugar maple stand," Adam said.

"Say again?" Nicolas's eyes followed the lustrous locks, which had just disappeared into the washroom.

"I bought myself a sugar maple stand," Adam said again, a bit louder this time.

In the pocket of his jacket, the vibration of his phone announced an incoming text message. *Have to go to Vancouver. Will call when I get there.* But because of the ambient noise and the exaggerated bass of the Serge Gainsbourg remix, Adam would only read the message several hours later as Marion, unable to doze off, stared at the night sky through the window of a plane flying over the Canadian prairies.

2008

IT WASN'T THAT SHE WAS ASHAMED OF THE MARK SHE'D gotten, but that she'd rather Mrs. Nelson hadn't announced it in front of the whole class. Did teachers think a student's excellent marks would improve their social standing? In what universe did they grow up? Celia wondered. More likely, as they grew older, they forgot that every achievement had to be paid for, in the best-case scenario by being jeered at in the hall, in the worst case, by run-of-the-mill threats and brutality, from the lunch that was commandeered in the cafeteria to the locker graffitied with insults. Hadn't Mrs. Nelson gone through the same thing, she whose passion for *Little Women* came out even in the clothes she chose to wear—lace-up high-heel boots, heavy woollen capes, and hand-knit bonnets edged in pale green velvet—leading to her daily lot of amused, superior glances from the school's fashionistas? Those girls had not yet realized that what they considered to be their fashion expertise revealed nothing more than their perfectly conventional adherence to the codes in force on the east coast and a habit of confusing money with personality.

*One day they'll know better,* mused Celia with a touch of ill will, *and when that day comes, they'll be hurt and full of shame.*

Actually, Mrs. Nelson may well not have clued into what others thought of her. Celia sometimes bumped into her on Saturdays in the bookstore her husband ran, a man so tall and skinny that Celia imagined him folding up like a letter to slide into a car. Mrs. Nelson, all curves and twirling skirts, helped him with the shelving or at the cash register, and whenever she saw Celia, she'd welcome her with the insistent warmth of those who had no children yet not for lack of trying.

They seemed happy together.

Back home from school, Celia quietly left her research paper on the kitchen table, *The Wampanoag: Martha's Vineyard's First People,* along with the A+ written in bold red letters by Mrs. Nelson, and a single comment: *Phenomenal!* She'd thought she'd tell her family over dinner. Sometimes she'd come up with things to say over supper in advance to keep the conversation from flagging and to entertain her mother. But after Mrs. Nelson's announcement, the shrill laughter of her classmates—what a misnomer, not a one was her "mate," not since Jodie had moved away the year before—she no longer felt like celebrating her mark, another excellent academic result to add to her pile of excellent academic results, a store of bricks with which to build the edifice of her ascension.

That's what Jeffrey maintained, he who would finish high school this year and had a university scholarship, thanks to football, an anomaly in their family of asthmatic confectioners.

"Brick by brick, Celia."

Whenever he said those words with his high-octane self-confidence, Celia made fun of him. "Yah, yah, Care Bear," she'd retort, "everything'll be just fine."

Lately, her mother had been tired. Or more tired than usual. Winters she worked in the supermarket, where she took on as many hours as possible so she could devote her time to the taffy shop at the end of May when tourist season started. Students replaced her in the supermarket, and when they left the island for the new school year, she returned. Celia didn't like the place much, with its stark lighting and smell of frozen foods. But Rhonda laughed as she talked to the other cashiers and it was good to hear. It might have been because of her father's recent visit, too. That was often the way of it when Julian came to see them: at the time, the family delighted in his stories from the other side of the world and in the rare record albums he'd bring back for them. But when he headed out again, each of them would retreat to his or her respective bedroom for days on end. It had been three weeks since he'd left, and it was as though Rhonda was still having a tough go of it.

Since Grandpa Herb's death a year ago, Rhonda had been looking pale. Celia heard her tell a friend over the phone that if she couldn't manage to keep the shop, it would be one blow too many. Her friend must have said something like *We shall overcome* because Rhonda added, "Let's hope so, let's hope so."

It was surprising to see Rhonda go to the mainland that day. "I'll be back late tonight. I've got some shopping to do on the mainland," she'd said in a voice that sounded weary to Celia. "You two'll have to look after getting supper together." It must be an important errand for her to miss a day's worth of work. Christmas shopping, maybe? The holidays were only three weeks away, so that must be it.

Putting water on to boil for hot dogs, Celia grimaced. The island was in a bad way, several neighbours' houses had sported FOR SALE signs for months now and some had been repossessed by the bank. Her neighbourhood wasn't the only one affected either. On the bus ride to school, she'd seen similar signs everywhere, even in front of the smart summer homes with their pastel walls. The news labelled it "the worst economic crisis since the Great Depression." *The Great Depression.* Every time Celia heard the expression, the image that sprang to mind was of a body face down in the sand, its head limp, its pupils empty, waves washing over it with each rising tide.

When she'd asked him if things were bad, her brother said, "Our new president will fix it."

Deep down, she had a streak of cynicism that had been steadily growing since birth. Celia would rather have inherited the other streak, her brother's. A streak of hope.

They were finishing supper when Rhonda walked in with a heavy tread. Celia felt as though she could *hear* the tension in her mother's muscles. Seeing her children at the table, Rhonda gave a strange, crooked smile, and when she said, "There you are, my babies," her voice sounded like the shifting of a seabed.

She told them she was off to have a shower.

Celia reminded her their TV show was on that evening. Her mother shook her head; wasn't it losing its appeal? The story had been stretched too thin.

They'd watched the series, a grating comedy, since day one. Back then, Celia had been too little to understand it all, but she loved to laugh out loud with Rhonda at the more humorous segments.

"You're right, it's not as good as it used to be," Celia lied, unsure what it was that made her feel like crying.

Just then Rhonda noticed Celia's assignment on the end of the table and raised her hand to her heart. "I've given birth to geniuses," she laughed, without the slightest hint of mockery.

Later, when Celia knocked on the door to her mother's bedroom, a hot dog in her hand—she had to be hungry, didn't she? Maybe that was it?—Rhonda lay stretched out on the bed in her bathrobe, her hands lying calmly on her stomach, like a child waiting for instructions.

"There's one hot dog left," Celia said.

"Leave it on the table, thanks, sweetheart," her mother replied.

"Aren't you hungry?"

"Not right now."

"Would you like some tea?"

"I'm okay."

"I'll let you be, Mom."

Then Rhonda opened her arms. They looked like they were so heavy. Yet there was no doubt—they were opened wide. Celia climbed in next to her and nestled her head against the soft, worn ratteen of the bathrobe by her shoulder.

"Are you tired?" Celia asked.

Rhonda swiped discreetly with the back of her hand at her eye. If you blot it out before it hits the ground, it never existed.

"A bit, sweetheart."

When, after several minutes of unmoving silence, she felt her mother's arm go limp and her breathing become slow and regular, Celia closed her eyes as well.

# The Sugaring Off

# 14

THAT SPRING WAS SHAPING UP TO BE IDEAL FOR THE SUG-
aring off, Sylvain had said, and now Adam said the same to
Marion, who stood before him in the shack like someone he
didn't know.

Yet she hadn't changed, her hair had the same lustre, so pale
it was almost transparent, and fell to below her chin in the
square cut he'd always known. She had slipped on one of Adam's
shirts, too big, a flannel affair in black-and-red plaid, the kind
you find in hardware stores by the gumboots and hunting caps,
but which Adam had bought online from a Nashville boutique
and paid something like three hundred dollars for—there were
shipping and customs fees, too; ethical consumption was expensive. She'd stuffed her hands deep in the pockets of her overalls
and stared at Adam, waiting for his instructions.

She was beautiful. Increasingly so.

Adam wanted to tell her how magical she looked in the
morning light, the scent of melting snow outside blending
with the fragrance of the wood stove, tell her he'd never stopped
loving her and that he had no explanation for the distance that
had grown between them—but he didn't.

He'd tried to have the same conversation a few months earlier, when she came back from Vancouver the day after New Year's, her eyes tired and her hair flattened on one side of her head from a night spent on the plane.

He'd said, "Did I do something?"

She shook her head. "No, you did nothing."

"Is it because we don't have a child?"

At that, she grew visibly annoyed. "Oh, give me a fucking break, all of you."

And so, on that score, she put him in the same boat as her parents and women's magazines: those who lumped all women together. Don't box me in, he understood. Don't box me in, he felt like replying.

"Is it because of Adèle?" he ventured next.

"Not that either," she answered. "Your daughter's home is here."

"So, what is it then?"

So, what is it then? he'd insisted.

And Marion's shrug was so weary that Adam felt himself break inside and he held his tongue.

Then she said, in a voice so weak he had to move closer to hear, "You were about to leave for the maple stand for some firewood, go on. I'll have a nap, go on."

And Adam left. Actually, he couldn't wait to go, the wood was just an excuse. Which Marion might have known. In the car, he turned on the radio and heard a report on a horticultural co-op in Abitibi and it made him think of his sister.

"You could have come here," Manue had said over the phone when he was at the Sweets' on Christmas Eve. Her voice held no reproach. It wasn't even a piece of advice, just a simple observation: Adam could have gone to Abitibi to spend Christmas with his sister if Marion's absence troubled him so.

Adam kept switching the phone from one hand to the other, then stuck his right hand deep in his coat pocket. His gloves must have fallen somewhere when he went outside to take the call, grabbing his coat on the way. The air behind the elder Sweet's house had a bite to it and the perfume of woodsmoke.

"Didn't have the energy for a trip," Adam said laconically, with the half-formulated hope that his sister would notice what a pitiful state he was in.

He hoped to hear her add how demoralized he must feel at Marion's sudden, unexplained desertion and how mean it was of her to leave him alone for Christmas. Shouldn't she at least have waited for Adèle to leave for her mother's place? Didn't she know how much he needed her?

However, since Manue had no idea just how much Adam needed Marion, there was no point expecting her to defend him. Manue didn't play that role in her brother's life. Their relationship was confined to the vague solicitude they expressed for each other by getting in touch four or five times a year, the cement a shared rancour toward their mother. Memories of the two of them as children brought a lump to Adam's throat and he massaged his neck to move nostalgia along. He never brought those days up with her.

"How's Claire?" Adam asked, since it was the right thing to do.

"She's thrown her back out," Manue answered, "and is acting like I'm her servant."

141

Adam could hear the fondness in his sister's voice and it made him jealous.

Yet he had no desire to be anywhere but where he was. The Sweets had lived up to their surname by inviting Adam and his children for Christmas dinner the minute Adam mentioned Marion's trip. Of course, the children backed out. It was the first time in a decade that the holidays had not gone according to the traditional plan. Every Christmas Eve, the children were expected at Sarah's, and on the twenty-fifth, Adam could take them to Marion's parents' house. The schedule had never varied, except during those winters when Sarah's parents had organized a holiday down south for the whole family, and, as a consequence, Adam and Marion put up with Raymond and Gisèle complaining about *all the food* that would go to waste and *all the gifts* they'd hoped to give to the children in person. Adam would then slip out onto the balcony for a smoke with his sister-in-law, who was delighted to no longer be the only one who made her parents suffer. He laughed along with her and didn't give it a second thought.

"Speaking of which, I've got to go, her Highness is waiting for her kir."

Adam pictured Manue and Claire in the living room of their house on the shores of the Harricana River, stretched out on a crocheted blanket, doing back exercises amid gales of laughter. Had he ever been that close to anyone? Actually, were they really that close or was what he felt distorted by the prism of his envy?

After he hung up, he went back inside, was told to close the door, no point heating the outdoors. The Sweets had waited for him to start the family poker tournament. Line offered him a glass of red wine, not wine from the full crate he'd brought with him, a delightful organic nectar, but a heavy Australian Syrah that Adam would never have considered if he'd seen it on the liquor store's shelves. They'd put his case in the pantry and might bring it out later, once everyone was drunk already and unable to taste a thing. Adam tried to think of a way to get rid of the plonk so he could open one of his own bottles, but he couldn't come up with a scenario that wouldn't end up with him insulting them. He raised the glass to his lips and thought, *No matter, I love being here, surrounded by my sisters.*

He let the words settle deep in his chest. *My sisters.*

ADAM OBEYED MARION'S REQUEST, FORGOT ABOUT CHRIST-mas, Manue, and the Syrah, and spent all afternoon tinkering in the shack. That evening, Marion curled up next to him on the couch and he thought she might want him.

He told himself, *This is your chance, it's always been easier for the two of you to speak through your bodies rather than words, quit being afraid.* For some time now, things hadn't been working that well in the libido department for him, he hadn't felt the urge for months now, not for her, not even alone in the shower, whereas before that had been part of his routine, a sort of complement to washing up. Well now, no, he was blocked, he'd start thinking about something else and kick himself for it: Did thinking of something else mean he'd never get it up again? All the agitation wasn't good for hard-ons, and when-ever he did try, he ended up losing his erection: over time, he found the whole business demoralizing, so it was easier to not even try. It was a surer bet.

So that evening on the couch he told himself, *Please, Adam, stop thinking, this is a matter of life or death*, but Marion didn't reach down for his fly, just laid her head on his shoulder, wrapped her arms round his elbow, then said, "Do you want to watch our series? The third season's just started."

They'd been following a couple of surly female investigators from the north of England track down the assholes heading up a child prostitution ring. Adam was relieved. Today, he wondered whether he'd made a mistake.

When he thought back to that night, he saw himself like one of the matchstick men in the *New Yorker*'s pencil cartoons, at a crossroads, his hands in his pockets, his shoulders slightly stooped, not knowing which road to take.

Had he taken one road and Marion another? Or had she simply abandoned him? After all, he was the one suffering, the one who'd just about died, the one who'd had to take stock of his failures as a parent and keep assuming his role as the pillar of the family without any support. On top of which, was it really up to him to shoulder the blame for the distance separating them? It wasn't like he was the one who'd fled to the other side of the country. He'd stayed put, his two feet planted on the frozen ground of their deserted property.

They had tried to go on as before, to act like a couple the way you'd orchestrate a Christmas dinner. Bubbly, gravlax, the children's presents, turkey, the adults' presents, yuletide log, after-dinner drinks. They'd done the shopping, bought new sheets, and accepted invitations to dinner, although their heart wasn't really in it.

Ten days earlier, they hadn't said a word on the drive to visit Simon and Julie. Neither Adam nor Marion felt like enduring the fifty-some-kilometre ride that separated Hudson from their friends' apartment in Notre-Dame-de-Grâce, but the couples hadn't seen each other since that summer and neither of them could come up with a good excuse for turning down the invitation. Not that the house wasn't to their liking. Every time, Marion told Julie how much she loved the warmth of their little love nest furnished with such good taste, and the ease with which the three of them shared the confined space while she and Adam had felt the need to build a house four times the size without even a child to raise.

Before they set out, Adam heard Marion knock on Adèle's door to offer her a plate of gnocchi reheated in the microwave. His daughter turned it down yet thanked her, and Adam thought to himself, *Adèle's doing better*, and couldn't help but hear Sarah erupt in his head: if showing basic courtesy is enough to make people celebrate the state of someone's mental health, then she herself was Mother Teresa.

As for Adam, he had chosen to look on the bright side and clung to that as much as possible. Of course, Adèle rarely left her room since she'd rather spend long days embroidering militant messages on a piece of fabric stretched over a hoop, which she then sold online. Sayings in English for the most part, *Nevertheless, She Persisted* or *Abortion Is Health Care*. Her feminist crafts were a hit in the U.S. and in English Canada. Recently, she'd also sold one she'd embroidered with small poppies and the inscription *Décrisse de mon utérus*, so she hadn't totally neglected the francophone market. Her trip to Thailand, which had meant so much to her that she'd dropped out of school, had inexplicably fallen by the wayside. "You should be proud to see me going into business instead," she'd said, offended when Adam teased her about it. Of course, no part of her business was profitable and, given the rate at which Adèle embroidered, she would never be able to make a living from it. However, over the months, her stubborn silence had morphed into a sort of distracted indifference. It was what one might call progress.

Adam loved Adèle the way he loved Simon and Julie: despite the distance. He had rarely spoken to his friend since last summer, avoiding tennis games, hockey tickets, and the liquid lunches Simon suggested. He had actually thought about inviting him to the maple stand and accepting his help during the sugaring off. He had thought about it but never followed through. Sylvain was there to help him, after all, even though his enthusiasm had waned since his father's hospitalization—yes, Mr. Sweet had just about died, but no, in the end he'd rallied and his daughters were taking turns at his bedside, which seemed a bit much to Adam, to tell the truth, given all there was to do for the sugaring off. Simon's presence might have pushed Sylvain even further away. Why intrude on the precious moments that lay ahead of them with endless explanations his city friends wouldn't understand, anyway? Because they understood nothing.

"You should park on Sherbrooke," Marion said as they left the Décarie Expressway. "You need a parking pass on all the side streets."

The prolonged period of not speaking had made her hoarse and she had to cough twice to clear her throat.

Just as they were about to get out of the car, she laid her hand on Adam's in an impulsive gesture and they clasped their joined fingers without looking at one another.

Philomène had something to tell them, Simon declared, almost before he'd finished pouring their drinks: his daughter had a drawing hidden behind her back, one she'd made to illustrate the surprise, and, before anyone could open their mouth, Marion said, "Julie's pregnant," and everyone, including Marion, winced.

Not at the news, which wasn't all that surprising, after all, but because of Marion's curtness, depriving the child of the pleasure of announcing the most defining—and the happiest—event of her short life.

Julie stared at Marion.

"What a party pooper," Simon blurted out.

Philomène looked from her father to her mother, the way children do when they've fallen and don't know yet whether they should cry. Marion felt the weight of Julie's disappointment on her and blushed. As for Adam, he broke into a huge smile, knelt down beside Philomène, and pretended not to have heard a thing.

"What did you want to tell us, Philo?"

Philomène pulled out the picture from behind her back, its figures drawn in felt pen: a blue man, a little green girl, and a red woman with a yellow circle filled with small pink hearts on her belly.

Adam's eyes widened. "Are you telling me you're going to be a big sister?"

Philomène nodded, happy but shy, then Simon laughed and welcomed Adam's excited hug; Julie dried a tear before helping herself to a glass of non-alcoholic cider.

Marion apologized again and again to Julie, who kept saying, "No problem, no problem, Marion, everyone steals a punchline now and then," and Adam thought, *Not Marion, not my woman.*

"IS THIS WHERE YOU'LL SLEEP?" SHE ASKED, HER EYES SURveying the room in which the evaporator took up almost the entire space. "There's barely room to move."

Adam waved vaguely at the south corner of the shack where he planned to set up a camp cot when the flow of syrup was at its greatest in a couple weeks' time. Sylvain used to camp here before him and had volunteered to do the same again this year—*It's part of the job, boss*—but Adam turned him down; if he wanted to call himself a sugarer, then he had to act like one.

At first he laughed whenever the elder Sweet used the term. Every time, he imagined a small cut-glass white sugar bowl with a tiny spoon and a delicate lid like the one his grandmother Dumont would set down on her lace openwork table runner after holiday meals. But no one other than tax collectors and news commentators used the term *maple sugar producer*; it was awkward, such a cold title to describe a job that was so—Adam didn't dare say instinctive since he didn't even know how to go about tapping his own maple trees—alive, let's say. Plus, ever since his father's hospitalization, Sylvain had seemed distracted and spent less time than planned in the sugar bush.

Adam didn't want to make a big deal out of it—what kind of man would he be to blame his employee for wanting to be with his father during the last months of his life? Marie, Nathalie, and Line continued to look after the elder Sweet as well, and Adam had noticed that they took longer calling him back when he phoned about such-and-such a use of the syrup, the taffy, or the sugar.

The day before, seized by a growing sense of vertigo at the thought that none of them would be there for the last day of tapping, he left four messages for Sylvain—not that he'd counted, but Nathalie did, and when she called him back late in the day, she said, "Adam, you don't need to leave four messages, my brother heard the first one, he just didn't have time to answer, Papa's oxygen dropped again today and we had to monitor him closely, they thought they might send him back to intensive care. Was your question urgent?"

And Adam stammered that he'd just wanted to confirm whether Sylvain would actually be away for the last day of tapping: it hadn't been easy working on his own, and Sylvain had promised to be with him so he wouldn't make any mistakes, mistakes that could end up costing him, and should he hire someone else?

Nathalie sighed and Adam bit the inside of his cheek, maybe he'd gone too far asking if he should hire someone else. For starters, he had no desire to do that and, moreover, he wouldn't have known where to look. The Sweets were his only contact. His guilt came with rising anger. Did they not understand how much he depended on them?

"I'm sure you'll be okay," Nathalie said finally in a disgruntled tone. "Ask your girlfriend—she drills teeth, she can drill trees just as easily."

He heard someone laugh behind her and recognized Line. He felt a tightness in his chest. Should he have gone to the hospital, too? If it was hard for him not being with them, maybe he should just go there? After all, the tapping could likely wait a few days more, long enough for Mr. Sweet to be on the mend, and then they'd return to the maple stand together and finish the job, happy and relieved.

He didn't have time to make the offer because Nathalie had to hang up: the on-call doctor had stepped into the room to give them an update; as everyone knows, an on-call doctor dropping by is as rare as Halley's Comet, and she ended the conversation there.

So today, here he stood before Marion, who awaited his instructions. He felt as awkward as a twelve-year-old boy asking a girl to the movies.

"Let's go outside," he finally uttered. "I'll show you."

Sylvain had said, "A notch is a wound. That's why the way you tap into the tree is so important. Actually, untapping is even more critical, since you can rip off bits of bark if you use too much force, and afterward it takes years to scar over, then the tree dies inside before you even know it, and, the first thing, it stops producing water. You owe it to your tree to make a proper wound. It sounds funny put like that, but that's the way it is. You have to wound it for the sugaring off. If you do it right, it will slowly heal, then you'll choose the safest spot for the next notch to let the old one heal, understand? It's a cycle. You create each new tap hole just far enough from the old one, that way they'll all keep on cohabiting and producing. Your drill bit makes a difference, too. You want a clean tap hole, you don't want to be chipping away left and right and cause all kinds of small hurts, understand? You measure your angle, twice, three times if necessary, you adjust your drill bit, you take your time. Whenever you set out to wound your tree, never forget that. It's like the slaughter on a farm. Necessary but violent. People don't like to think of the violence that goes into their barbe-cued chicken thigh, and I get it, I don't like violence any more than the next person. But that's what your tree asks of you: to be careful because you know it will hurt."

Adam repeated for Marion's benefit what Sylvain had taught him. As he spoke, he realized it was hard for him to look her in the eye; his gaze settled almost anywhere except on her: on the blue tubes strung from one tree to the next in a slack curve. On a plane, high in the sky. On his snowshoes, which Marion wore.

She hadn't brought her own, even though he'd asked her to, so he loaned her the ones Sylvain had told him to buy in Jan-uary when Adam showed up in the woods on cross-country skis. He hadn't even been able to make it three metres. The trees were too tightly packed, the terrain steep. "What a city-boy plan," Sylvain guffawed.

Adam's snowshoes were too big for Marion. He'd knelt in front of her, his gloves between his teeth, to tighten the laces as far as they'd go. Now he stared at the snow accumulating between the sole of her boot and the snowshoe and spoke to her of a maple tree's hidden wounds, recognizing the many metaphors for love as numerous as rivulets come spring, which was probably why he couldn't look her in the eye. What a strange sensation to have forgotten how to gaze into eyes one knows better than any others.

Ultimately, it was easier to say nothing at all, and they spent the day tapping the trees in silence. When darkness fell, they were done.

# 15

THE PLUMBER BURST INTO THE CLINIC'S WAITING ROOM, making a beeline for Suzanne just as she held up her palm to stop him.

"Those blue slippers aren't just there for show." She nodded at the basket of disposable hospital slippers put there for patients during the winter months—and March counted as part of winter, at least given the state of the sidewalks and streets outside, everyone knows that.

The plumber, a man so tall he'd had to bow his head to enter through the doorway, backed up but didn't take a pair of slippers. He simply stood on the threshold. There'd been no answer on the next floor up.

"I thought Dr. Atallah went up with you."

The man shrugged, not knowing who Suzanne meant. The secretary who scheduled appointments, a sad woman whose name was Mélissa and who brought her colleagues inedible energy balls they discreetly rid themselves of to avoid making her any sadder, told her that Claude, excuse me, Dr. Atallah— Mélissa avoided any sign of a lack of respect toward her bosses—was eating out today and had not yet returned.

Suzanne sighed and stood up grudgingly to knock on the door to Marion's consultation room.

"Sorry to interrupt you, Dr. Robert. The plumber's here."

"And?" said Marion as she finished injecting local anesthetic into a patient's gums.

"And the tenant isn't in," added Suzanne, and in a faintly sarcastic tone, enough for Marion to hear without alerting the patients, "and Dr. Atallah is *eating out*."

Marion smiled behind her surgical mask. *Eating out* was the code word given to the couples counselling that Claude and his young wife attended to *prepare in unison for the transition to the retirement of one member of the duo*, read their shrink's website. Suzanne had shown the description to Marion after Claude told her he would like to block off his lunch hour for the next three Wednesdays.

Suzanne rolled her eyes: the duo would have time, money, leisure activities, and travel to spare, and if Audrey wanted to stop working for good, she had only to say the word: God give them the strength to weather such an ordeal. Marion laughed slightly and asked Suzanne not to show the site to anyone else, and Suzanne was hurt to think Marion didn't know that she kept any such malicious gossip for her ears only.

At the time, Marion had made herself a promise: *Tonight Adam and I will have a good laugh over this, how idiotic, the quintessence of blind privilege*, then she remembered they no longer laughed together over things like that, and she pushed to the back of her mind the unpleasant conviction that she herself represented a certain blindness to privilege in someone else's eyes.

As she told her patient it would be a few minutes before the anesthetic took effect, Marion removed her gloves and mask and followed Suzanne into the waiting room. Jessie watched as she walked out and, instinctively, Marion bowed her head like a penitent. Ever since her boss had failed to show up for her wedding, which in the end was celebrated on Valentine's Day, Jessie had tried hard to behave normally, but their every exchange hinted at her disappointment and the fragile hope that Marion would say something to make up for her transgression. Marion had apologized profusely: "I left Montreal too late, but with the storm making the roads through the Laurentians almost impassable, I had to turn back, I'm so sorry I missed it, Jessie." She'd given the same speech so many times it had become an actual song with its own chord progression, its choruses. A bit of fiction, in Jessie's view: the storm only started late in the day while the welcome cocktail for the wedding had been set for three o'clock. If the storm had blocked Marion, that meant she'd started out just as Jessie and Kevin were exchanging their vows, a good hour later.

The storm wasn't the only factor to blame for her absence. Marion had been negligent, she had not taken this important event in Jessie's life seriously, and why hadn't she agreed to stay at the inn the night before like the rest of her loved ones, the ones who'd made the effort? Marion had disappointed her. And the situation so upset her that, when she received Marion's contrite text in the middle of the reception—a text in response to the half-dozen worried messages she herself had sent—her only reply was a happy face and two sentences: *No big deal. I'll keep a slice of cake for you.* The cake was presented to her the following week, when Jessie returned from her honeymoon in Mexico, a frozen slice in a worn plastic container. To Marion as she took it from Jessie, it felt as heavy as an anvil.

"You shouldn't have," said Marion, and although it was a common expression of courtesy, she couldn't help noticing that that was exactly how she felt: *You shouldn't have brought me this offering, this offering points at my guilt, this offering is a punishment. You shouldn't have expected anything from me.*

She apologized again and made Jessie promise she'd show her the pictures and videos of the ceremony. Jessie nodded with a smile but still had not shown them to her a month later. In the end, Marion acknowledged that, in all honesty, the distance between them suited her. Of course, at some point, the abscess would have to be lanced, but who knows? With a bit of luck, Jessie would rather find another job than pour her heart out.

A small puddle of melted snow had formed under the plumber's feet and a thread of grey water ran between the floor tiles. Suzanne glared at the man as she returned to her spot behind the counter.

Marion explained that a wet, slightly brownish stain had appeared the day before on the ceiling of their washroom and had been growing ever since. A small bubble had formed and threatened to penetrate the paint.

"Shall I show you?" Marion asked as she headed for the washroom.

Obliged to enter, the plumber cast a glance at the blue slippers, then stepped out of his boots without bending over, working away at the heels.

It was in the washroom that Marion noticed how tall he was. Basketball tall, Dutch tall. He didn't even need to raise his chin to see the stain, and he prodded the bubble on the ceiling as easily as he would have turned the doorknob.

"It's coming from upstairs," he said. He coughed, perhaps embarrassed to announce something so obvious.

Did he think they didn't know that? That's why Suzanne had spoken of the tenant. Marion felt like saying as much, but the voice she heard in her head sounded like her sister's voice speaking to people she held in disdain. Marion hated that tone, so all she said was "Let's go, my partner keeps the tenant's keys somewhere."

"I could've smashed the door in, but I didn't think your boss would've approved," said the seven-foot plumber jokingly.

"He's not my boss," Marion replied.

She'd meant to go to Jessie's wedding, enough to shower, anyway, do her hair, take her accordion-pleated red dress out of the closet, the one she'd only worn once the year before at the reopening of a luxury hotel with a renowned American chef—Adam had been witty all night long, sailing from one conversation to the next and had waltzed magnificently, his hand on the small of her back, happy and radiant. After examining herself in her large bedroom mirror, Marion saw no difference compared to that night—the same dress, the same face, *and yet*. She applied her makeup with care and slipped into a cotton bag the high heels she would wear later at the wedding. She called out to Adam in the bathroom: it was time to go if they didn't want to be late. Adam didn't answer right away and Marion heard the water running, a continuous stream, the soundtrack to his secret crying jags, and didn't even bother insisting. "Get some rest, I won't stay long."

Adam managed to murmur, okay, it was better that way, he wouldn't have been good company in any case.

She didn't turn off at the Laurentian Autoroute but followed the route to downtown instead, where she walked in the shadow of its tall office towers. Night had fallen abruptly; she was cold. Crowds of passersby formed around her; they were all heading to the same place. Their cheerful voices contrasted with their bowed heads struggling against the blowing snow. Marion let herself be carried along by the moving tide, in the heart of the crowd making for the hockey game between Montreal and Philadelphia. She bought a ticket on the street from a twangy-sounding scalper and sat on a blue foldaway seat to watch players the size of ants as they skated. She drank beer from a plastic cup and ate a hot dog, dripping mustard onto her dress. Every time the Canadiens scored a goal, she jumped up to yell and she laughed with her seatmates, four cousins in their fifties come from Drummondville for the game, an annual tradition. Afterward, she'd taken her time leaving, not trying to avoid the spectators thronging the halls and stairways. On the trip back, the roads were icy and she saw two cars in the ditch.

"How was it?" asked Adam sleepily when she got home.

"Great," she said.

The upstairs tenant must be away on a trip; she hadn't come to the door or answered the messages the clinic had been leaving since the previous day. That was surprising since most people check their phones non-stop, even from the other side of the world. Didn't she know that cellphone providers now offered advantageous data-use programs abroad? Marion mulled over those thoughts as she climbed the stairs with the plumber behind her. Maybe the upstairs tenant was the kind who retreated to a spartan cottage deep in a forest without running water or cell reception, and, if that was the case, she was more interesting than she seemed with her inevitable yoga outfit and little apple-green car.

Just in case, Marion knocked. She thought back to her own disappearance over Christmas. Her sister hadn't put her up in a cottage deep in the woods, and yet, for several days, she had failed to respond to the (many) calls from her parents and to those (few) from her partner. Did that make her interesting, however?

She shrugged, as much in self-mockery as to show the plumber they'd waited long enough and she was ready to open the door.

The apartment was decorated without a hint of originality, yet the effect at first glance was a pleasing one. An honest stab at the chic boho look with its sofa upholstered in fuchsia velvet and its fake-worn Persian rug. To hide the kitchen's beige backsplash that Claude had had changed in the late nineties and wasn't about to renovate any time soon, the tenant had laid adhesive vinyl tiles in various patterns reminiscent of traditional Portuguese azulejos. Had the neighbour been there, Marion would have said, "Oh! How pretty your place is," and it wouldn't have been a lie.

Not a total lie in any case.

The plumber didn't linger to admire the effect. He did notice, however, through the living-room window the white bicycle perched on its tree, and made the sign of the cross before continuing.

"I've found the culprit," he now said, loud enough for her to understand he was speaking to her.

The small sink in the bathroom was overflowing. A rivulet trickled down to the wall, where the baseboard's quarter round, swollen with moisture, let the water into the floor structure that gave onto the clinic's ceiling. The tap dripped once every second, which kept the whole merry-go-round turning.

A disposable razor had been left on the edge of the sink. In the water full of soap scum, a multitude of small dark hairs floated on the surface. The sink's drain stopper had been lowered and someone—the tenant, obviously—had forgotten a pink wash-cloth there. Marion saw the scene with almost disturbing acuity.

She could see her—the girl with the patterned leggings—her foot on the ratteen terry towel so as not to get anything wet, shaving her leg from ankle to knee. Tap-tapping on the edge of the sink to knock the hairs off, then sticking the razor back under the hot water and starting all over again. Something had interrupted the operation. A girlfriend's call for help, a text message from her elusive lover announcing he was breaking up with her, bad news about her mother. Death. Someone else's, obviously, since the apartment was empty.

Unless she'd been assaulted? Marion imagined a man creeping up on her from behind, throwing his arm round her neck, dragging her into the bedroom. But there would be traces of violence, wouldn't there? Isn't that what the newspapers wrote to imply a suspicious death?

The expression *traces of violence* was uncommon, almost poetic. Was there anything at all in this world that didn't bear traces of violence? Being passed on the right on the highway. The school picture with its commands to smile. The family itself—good god!—was paint-spattered with violence. Didn't it take an idiot—or at least someone intensely naive—to believe that it was enough to see no trace of violence for violence to be considered absent?

"I'm not afraid of you, but you should be afraid of me!" a voice cried from the entrance.

From where he knelt beneath the sink, the plumber switched off his flashlight and glanced over at Marion.

Had someone really spoken? Or was Marion the only one to have heard a message meant for her, a motto, *I'm not afraid of you, but you should be afraid of me,* the phrase said it all, didn't it, everyone considered Marion's niceness a sign of blandness, they had no idea it was a weapon, *you should be afraid of me*: she couldn't have said it better herself, that was it exactly.

"There's someone here," said the plumber, and Marion turned and peered out from behind the door. At the end of the hallway, a woman, her hair long and loose, wearing an electric-mauve down jacket, stood waiting.

"I'm Marion—Dr. Robert. I'm Dr. Atallah's partner. Our bathroom ceiling is leaking, and it's coming from your bathroom. We've been trying to call you since yesterday, but you haven't been answering. We had no choice but to enter. Is everything all right?"

The tenant opened her eyes wide as though this was the first time anyone had asked that question. As she approached, Marion saw the woman was much older than she'd thought. Her face, almost coppery, had been exposed to thousands of hours of sunshine, and white roots showed under her light-brown hair. Well into her sixties, decided Marion, astonished at her mistake. From a distance, stepping into or out of her car, her yoga mat strapped to her back, the woman had looked so energetic, so *young*.

"Everything's fine," she answered. "I just went out for a walk."

Marion frowned. "It's been leaking since yesterday."

Hearing those words, the tenant cast around as though searching for an excuse, a lifeline. She had the look of someone who'd just been caught stealing oranges in a grocery store.

"It's been raining since the deluge," she replied, and Marion took a deep breath. Under her winter jacket, the tenant wore cycling shorts. One leg was closely shaved, the other not. She wore no socks and the laces on her runners were undone.

"Can you tell me your name?" asked Marion.

"What, you think I've forgotten my name? I'll have you know I have never, not once, forgotten my name. Maybe my keys, maybe where I parked the car, or the time for an appointment, but what of it? Is that what really matters? I'm Odette Cohen and I've known who I am since the day I was born."

Marion stood rooted to the spot, at a loss for words. It was the plumber who spoke.

"The thing is, you've gotta shut the tap off when you go out."

The tenant burst out laughing, as though the plumber had said the most adorable and appropriate thing imaginable.

Marion could already hear her telling her children (did she have children? Who would come to take care of this woman, lost and alone?) over and over, *and that's when the plumber said: The thing is, you've gotta shut the tap off when you go out.*

On her way back down to the clinic where her assistant had kindly kept a conversation going with the patient who'd been numb for the past twenty minutes, Marion stopped in the stairway, unable to catch her breath.

# 16

ADAM BROUGHT OUT THE GIN GLASSES, HIS BEST, THE heavy ones. He had stored them in their box, careful to insert cardboard in between so they wouldn't chip. On the table, he had laid out salami, spiced walnuts, flatbread cooked on the wood stove and a za'atar labneh dip. The shucked oysters lay on their bed of snow. Everything was ready.

Neither Sylvain nor his sisters had answered his text yet inviting them to the shack to celebrate the first real flow of maple sap. Adam had just had an ideal, exhilarating week gathering the maple water and boiling it down night and day. The syrup was bottled and the preserves were lined up on the shelves like a promise kept, a positive outcome. Whether it actually was or not, he didn't really ask himself. Sylvain had said *uh-huh*, climbing into his truck at the end of the day when Adam suggested they celebrate. He'd said *uh-huh* and closed the door with a screech of metal in need of oil, it wasn't an *okay*, it wasn't an *absolutely, with pleasure*, but it wasn't a *no* either; it wasn't an *in your dreams*. It was *uh-huh*.

He would come, his sisters would come.

Adam would serve them gin-and-sap liqueurs, he'd promised in his message, made with the hard-to-find Gaspé gin he'd managed to purchase through his restaurant DNA, and it would be his treat for their helping him and believing in him. They'd make plans for the following year, talk about expanding, Adam would propose that Sylvain become his partner—Marie, Nathalie, and Line, too, if they liked. The company would be called Mont Sweet, a natural combination of their names, Dumont and Sweet. A TV crew would follow their adventure, his producers couldn't wait—in actual fact, his producers had quit expecting much from him, other than that he finish his season of *Adam à table* in one piece and recuperate over the summer, but no use worrying the Sweets with that. He could already see their touched expressions, face flushed with the heat from the evaporator and the alcohol, nose shining, eyes moist. They would sing tunes from another era handed down by their ancestors and, in the early hours of the morning, they would teeter out into the dawn, shoulder to shoulder, to listen to the maple water flowing through the tubes.

It was already after eight o'clock, and Adam decided to pour himself his first glass of gin, just because. He'd had nothing to drink other than two beers at the end of the day and the few swigs of Scotch he allowed himself from time to time to keep warm.

Marion loathed flasks. A flask always held shame, she declared when he got one for his fortieth birthday, a far too expensive gift on which his partners had had his name engraved. He had shut the flask away in a desk drawer and totally forgotten about it till he started packing his bags for the sugaring off, eight years later.

Ever since, he'd kept it in his pants pocket, full of Glenfiddich. Whenever he slipped his hands into his pockets to warm them, he liked to stroke its perfectly smooth metal surface with his fingertip.

He took his first swig of gin straight up, savouring the burn of the liquid down his throat. Then he helped himself at the evaporator tap. The maple water hadn't yet been converted into syrup, but it had a deliciously high concentration of sugar, as warm as tea. The mix was tasty and soothing, a sort of grog, Sylvain had said, and he was right. Soon Adam's glass was too hot to hold in his bare hands; after downing its contents, he stored it away with the others in the cardboard box and brought out the stoneware cups. The Sweets would prefer them.

At nine-thirty, after downing two more mixes, two gins neat, and eating half the oysters on the platter, Adam still sat staring at his phone, which continued to refuse to bring him news of anyone.

*Are you coming soon?* he'd texted at 8:35.

*The oysters are getting warm!* he'd added at 9:00.

*I'm warning you, I'm eating one,* at 9:03.

*Three down, eighteen to go,* at 9:08.

He meant to amuse them, to make them laugh, convinced they'd arrive any second; as they walked into the shack, they'd holler to give him a start; they went in for pranks like that, didn't they?

But twenty-one minutes had gone by since his last text and no one had turned up at the door yet to surprise him.

He called Marion. Adam had to pull the phone away from his ear the minute she picked up because of all the background noise. Unpleasant.

"Where are you?"

"Oh, it's a wine bar, but I think it's a small pop-up kitchen, too. Someone's just brought me a basket of truly delicious cod fritters."

"Where?" Adam had trouble hearing her.

"With friends," Marion replied, adding, "from university, friends from university." Somewhat curtly it seemed to Adam. "Are you still at the shack?"

Behind her, he could hear music, voices calling out, a persistent bass line. What were they all laughing at? Adam asked, "What university friends?"

Marion burst out laughing. "Sorry, the waiters are really funny here."

Adam said nothing. Marion gave a little cough, she was having a hard time hearing him, she'd have to call back later.

"How about coming to join me here?" said Adam all of a sudden. "I've got gin, salami, you'd look beautiful in the glow from the wood stove."

It was Marion's turn to say nothing. Not for long, just two or three seconds before she stammered out that it was late and she was thinking of going home soon, anyway. She was exhausted.

"I'll come see you tomorrow, why don't I?" she said the way you promise your grandmother you'll visit her in the nursing home—in other words, in a falsely jovial tone. "I'll help you bottle the syrup."

Adam felt himself being engulfed in cold sand. He spoke at last, his voice icy and clipped. "No need, I've got my people here."

At ten-forty, Adam knocked on the door of the tired-looking farmhouse belonging to Gerry Sweet. He'd barely taken the time to lace up his boots and, coatless, stood shivering in his Irish-knit wool sweater. His ears were red from the trek between the shack and the little farmhouse. The bottle of gin in his left hand was almost empty.

"Hey, Sweets, be sweet, open the door, will you?"

Then he laughed, but not because it was funny. He knocked on the door, on the window, then on the door again. Lamps were still on, it was plain to see.

"Hey-oh!" he cried, and in the cold of the night his echo resounded pleasingly.

The door opened abruptly.

"Nathalie! I'm so glad to see you! It's a bit cold out, could I come in? I've got gin! Oops, I had some gin. No big deal, I've got my Scotch somewhere, let me rummage through my pockets."

Nathalie wrapped her cardigan round her. "This isn't a good time, Adam."

She wasn't smiling. Adam looked at her, waiting for her to continue. Or to break into laughter and slap him on the back, saying, *I'm just funning you, come on in, you big fool.*

"What's going on?" he articulated finally. His mouth felt pasty, he hated that sticky saliva sound.

Nathalie sighed. "Papa left us tonight."

Adam didn't catch on right away, he thought, *Left for where?* but just as he was about to say the words out loud, he saw, behind Nathalie's shoulder, Line and Sylvain seated at the table, and Sylvain was crying, his head between his hands. Everything drained away, he was a six-lane highway, totally deserted.

"But he was doing better!"

Adam spoke like a child who refuses to acknowledge bad news. Nathalie's gaze didn't soften.

"We'd like some family time," she said, and it wasn't a request.

Adam blinked several times.

"You should go back to yours."

The words were not spoken cruelly, but what difference did that make? The effect was unequivocal.

The door closed and Adam watched Nathalie walk away behind the curtain as not a single person looked in his direction. He circled the house to get a better view of the small dining room. Marie was there, too, rubbing her brother's back. Nathalie opened a bottle of beer and took a long swig. Sylvain looked at her and burst out laughing, followed by the other two sisters. Nathalie held the beer out to her brother, who drank from the bottle as well. Then Marie, then Line. Was it a pact? A memory? An inside joke, the supreme privilege of tight-knit families, as people who love each other are called?

Adam would never know what made them laugh that night, just that it could only take place in his absence, and that realization made him drop to the cold, bare ground of sugaring-off season.

# 17

MARION TOOK A FEW SECONDS TO FIGURE OUT WHERE she was.

The morning light filtered through a curtain patterned with flowers, oversize hydrangeas in bright colours. The sheets were a bit too soft for her liking. Brushed cotton? On the bedside table, a plastic trinket—a pale pink, chubby-cheeked rabbit—looked like the kind of balloon figure a clown makes during a kids' party.

Then it came back to her.

The tenant. She was in the tenant's apartment. She turned her head and saw, on the paisley yellow-and-ochre-patterned pillow, a head topped by black curly hair. Marion caught her breath.

She hadn't planned to go to the Faculty of Dentistry reunion, but, urged on by Yara, who was visiting Montreal at the time, she'd changed her mind. The reception was a dull affair in a room someone had booked downtown. It didn't take Yara long to figure out that, if they wanted an actual party, they'd have to go elsewhere.

Yara had just divorced a controlling husband who kept trying to wrest away custody of their two children and keep them from returning to Canada with her, harassing her with accusatory phone calls day and night, a horrific outcome that would have kept her trapped in Florida till the children reached adulthood. She was in dire need of a bender worthy of the name. They rounded up as many friends as they could to follow them to the Mile-Ex bar Adam had once taken Marion to, where she'd been struck by its clandestine and exhilarating edge.

Yara roped in Christian, whom Marion hadn't seen since university, not since the time they'd spent three days together without leaving their bed, just after graduation. When the three days were over, he'd promised to phone her the next day, once he'd had brunch at the chalet that his father, a TV quiz-show host, owned in Saint-Sauveur. Of course, he never did call. She'd always said she'd never been in love and had derived as much out of those crazy days as he did, including an amazing number of orgasms. All the same, knowing she would see him again fifteen years later, it would have done Marion good to see he hadn't aged well. He showed up, cheerful and sun-tanned as though just back from skiing, his hair as glorious as at the age of twenty, a curly mane, jet-black, slightly shorter now and streaked with grey. His heartfelt hug and the way he took Marion's face in his hands as he exclaimed, "God, I love that face," decided the matter: she would sleep with him.

She made the decision as casually as she chose a dish from the menu. Oh, gnocchi with sage butter and a carrot salad, yes, I'll have that please.

Ever since Patrick, instead of triggering remorse, taking the plunge had become second nature. There was now a window where once a wall had stood.

There'd been that jogger in Vancouver she'd followed home and who had left his door open. On her return, she'd announced to Myriam, "I've just given a blow job to one of your neighbours, his name is Jagur," and her sister laughed. "Cool. I've just sent a picture of my boobs to my colleague in human resources." The sisters had always found it easier to tell the truth in the guise of a joke, even though it was sometimes difficult to tell the difference between the two.

Myriam had been considerate, leaving it up to their parents to ask any questions. Gisèle phoned every day, trying to comprehend: How could Marion have left them alone over Christmas? Was her relationship in trouble? Was the clinic experiencing financial problems? Was Marion suffering from burnout because, if so, there was no reason to feel ashamed. "Annie, Mona's daughter, also suffered from exhaustion, you know, the one who teaches Grade 2; she's been on stress leave since October. The demands of today's world are too much, look at you: almost forty and you haven't even found time to have kids, and if you start now, it'll be too late, won't it? Marilyn, whose father is Luc, you know, the judge, your father's golf partner, she waited, too, and it never took; they had to go to a fertility clinic, and let me tell you, that's no picnic, Marion, you end up with bruises all over your belly and in a foul mood and you've barely got a thirty per cent chance of conceiving; next there's always adoption, but do you really want to go there? Those kids are a mess when they show up, and it's not to speak ill of anyone, but your precious Adam is too busy to deal with that, right? Why not take a break? Slow down a little, the clinic would still be there after your maternity leave, no one would steal it from you. Time, however, there's no getting that back. It trickles through your fingers like sand, hon, mark my words. Could you pass the phone to your sister? I have a few words for her, too."

Myriam, who'd heard the whole conversation over the speakerphone, made a few obscene gestures to get Marion to laugh, then she took over: "Hi, Maman, the time allotted for passing judgment on your children's lives is up; yes, I'm still with the same firm; no, I won't be going back to Quebec; no, I didn't make your favourite daughter drink a poisoned elixir to lure her over to the dark side. She's capable of making decisions all on her own like a big girl. Yes, I love you both, yes, hugs and kisses, we'll call on New Year's Day, bye."

Myriam threw the phone in the direction of the couch and they opened a bottle of wine.

"Why don't you ask me any questions?"

"It's not my style."

"I know, but…don't you wonder?"

"No need. You. Me." Myriam placed her index finger on Marion's solar plexus, then on her own. "We're a lot more alike than you think."

"I know. I know that now."

"It took a while."

"Had I known."

"What, had you known? What would you have done differently?"

"I don't know. I wouldn't have wasted as much time being…"

"Being a fucking doormat?"

Marion shrugged. "I love Adam, you know. I love everyone."

"That's not the question, moron."

"Right. That's not the question."

Later, Myriam received a call from her friend Kate and they went to a party at friends of friends in a house that had a solarium decorated with Tibetan flags. Marion smoked pot and kissed a girl, a redhead who wore her hair in two loose braids. She looked like Anne of Green Gables; *look at me tongue-kissing my childhood*, and Marion started to giggle.

After Vancouver, there'd been the barman at the hotel during her orthodontics course in Sherbrooke, who'd knelt before her in the shower.

Then John, a much younger baritone from the choir, surprisingly strong, given his thin, lanky body.

There'd been no problem going back to singing after what had happened in December. One night in the pub with the choir, emboldened by his inebriated state, Patrick asked Marion why she didn't want him anymore and what John had that he didn't.

She planted a tender kiss on Patrick's lips, *nothing at all*, and believed it. But she'd do better not to mix choir and coitus in future.

The opportunities grew fewer and further between during the depths of winter. No one goes out and there were so many layers to strip off to get naked that it allowed for a lot of time to change your mind. Occasionally, Marion went back to Adam when she got too horny or she missed him too much. But it saddened her, and he seemed so lost; the lover who used to shape her like dough now no longer knew where to lay his hands on her body or how to secure himself to her, and it was all such a downer. So she didn't go back there often.

With Christian, events unfolded the way she'd imagined them unfolding back in the day when she'd devoted an embarrassing amount of energy projecting herself into an eventual reunion: he told her she looked magnificent, expressed regret at *having let her get away.* Marion took note of that small act of cowardice on his part, did he think he could rewrite a past she had both witnessed and been part of? He'd struggled with—or made a pretence of struggling with—his conscience between midnight and the bar's closing, but surrendered in the face of Marion's *magnetic pull.* He couldn't invite her back to his place, where his wife slept without a care next to their three children—twins and their youngest little boy—and Marion didn't want to have him over to her place either. There he'd have seen the fabulous life she'd made for herself and felt jealous of Adam, and his regrets would have bolstered his interest. Adam was staying over at the maple farm; he wouldn't be home and even Adèle had left the house for a road trip to New York organized by her best friend.

"Generous of her," Marion conceded when Adèle told her that Léa's mother had given her daughter her old Subaru. Adèle was busy laying the clothes for her trip across the drying rack in the laundry room. The care she took with them was out of keeping with her negligence where any other household chore was concerned.

Adèle frowned. "What, you wouldn't have done the same?"

Lately, she'd bought even more second-hand T-shirts, with a particular penchant for tasteless promotional logos: the logo for the Quebec Order of Engineers, or the toucan mascot for an all-inclusive resort in Punta Cana. She wore them over bleached jeans or flowery skirts whose cut Marion found quite unflattering. That wasn't the goal; Adèle was ridding herself of the need to please others, of subservience. Her choice of clothing was deliberate. So Marion kept her comments to herself, which was something at least—better than Adam's bad jokes. "I can buy you new clothes if you want, you don't need to dress like a pauper."

Marion stared at length at Adèle before responding since she didn't know whether she would have given her car to her nineteen-year-old stepdaughter. She'd bought her first car in her twenties, after saving up the money she'd earned working as a camp counsellor nicknamed Rogue, who led excursions through the forest and shouted out call-and-response songs, summer after summer for five years. That had taught her the value of money and a job.

"Good God, I've turned into my father."

Adèle paused, pensive, still holding a damp, powder-blue fleece jacket. "How funny—no way can I imagine you as a camp counsellor."

Marion knew what that meant: You don't like children. You have no desire to have children, otherwise my father would have given you all kinds. A horde of little brothers would have followed me everywhere, worshipping me like the rock-star big sister I would have been. You'd have worried yourself sick every time I came home with a raging migraine instead of offering first aid with an impassive expression and the amused turn of phrase as I threw my guts up: "I think you'll survive." Mothers don't say that kind of thing, mine would never have said that, or at least not until recently. I would have listened to you talking to your girlfriends on the phone for hours about the effects of educational reform on what my generation was learning, and you'd have said stuff like "My stepdaughter's highly sensitive, she needs a teacher who can understand her," and you'd have gone on and on about Félix and me. You never did go on and on.

Adèle had had no need to say any of that, it was understood.

"You know what, sweetheart? I can't imagine you as a camp counsellor either!" was Marion's only reply as she shoved an armload of towels into the washing machine.

And Adèle understood that her answer was a slap in the face.

Then she left for New York. And Marion, not knowing whether it was her way of thumbing her nose at her stepdaughter or of apologizing, watched her leave through the French door the way a mother would.

It wasn't the first rule she'd flouted and, most likely, breaking and entering into the tenant's suite above the clinic to have sex was even more reprehensible than doing it under her own roof.

Something in Adam's voice when he'd called midway through the evening, a moan inaudible to anyone but her, cut too close to the bone. She was determined to take what she wanted; her spirit would no longer be curbed by anyone, and cracking the varnish of her supposed niceness made her deliriously happy. Yes, really, there was no turning back. She would never again ignore her instincts, no, she had been too starved for that to happen; she'd been taught to want nothing but the happiness of others—sickeningly so. Now, though, there was still that damn thread, the love she couldn't manage to supplant. You could learn how to take what you wanted, but it wouldn't stop you from suffering along with those you loved.

So, she told Christian, "Come with me, I know a place, the apartment's deserted, a sad story. The woman had to be put in a home, her nephew will be emptying it out soon, come with me, I've got the key."

He found the idea just transgressive enough to get an immediate hard-on.

Come morning, Marion watched this ordinary man with the face of an angel as he slept next to her. Her thoughts took her back to Odette Cohen—relieved that she'd remembered her name. What would become of her furniture, her travel guides sorted by region of the world in the living room's oak bookcase, her candy-pink yoga mat with the occasional smear of grey: traces of the bare feet of a woman whose final years would be spent between the suffocating walls of an assisted-living residence—a place one goes to die. Odette Cohen would know; she had spent thirty years bathing old people and getting them to swallow portions of puréed food. Or might her cognitive losses, which could only accelerate, shield her from taking the full measure of what lay ahead? Otherwise, how to explain her agreeing to be led to the slaughterhouse without screaming and pummelling her nephew, the staff, and whoever crossed her path? Why had she, after wandering through a park in the cold all one night with a half-shaven leg, decided to return home instead of fleeing so no one could dictate the terms of her ascension into oblivion?

Christian rolled over without waking. Marion was dying for the platter of eggs, bacon, potatoes, and pancakes they served in the restaurant across the street.

She didn't leave a note on her way out.

# 18

ONLY ONE MORE HOUR AND I'LL GO BACK TO THE LAND, Adam promised himself.

He'd taken to calling it *the land* rather than the sugar maple stand or shack. He liked the permanency of the designation that pointed to something bigger than a place, more lasting than property. There could be both a spiritual and macabre sense to *returning to the land, to the earth*—and you had to admit, that's what he, the good-time Charlie, the leading light of the best kitchens in the metropolis, the lover of food and flesh to touch or to taste, always the joker, was going through. That incorrigible Adam had morphed into damp, dark soil, teeming with worms and pitted with roots, a malleable, subservient matter, destined to die—or to be reborn.

He didn't even know if he was still suffering or if his anguish had been supplanted by resigned detachment, which has its own tragic potential, but a hint of the ridiculous, too.

He had jumped through the open door of an airplane and his parachute hadn't opened. Unlike his son, who loved the sport, he had never gone parachuting. Should he have? Had he failed in his duty to live life to the full, to see with his own eyes whether the sky was truly the limit? Was a secret hidden there, a key? He'd have to ask Félix. Now, for Adam, nothing but the earth made sense.

*Only one more hour and I'll go back to the land*, Adam told himself again as he knocked on the door of suite 307 inside a well-maintained building centrally located on Île des Sœurs, where his mother lived.

A few seconds later, his mother opened the door. He could have just walked in; it wasn't locked, and to open it she had had to get up from the other side of the apartment with her bad back. This might be news to him since he rarely asked after her health. The whole of Île des Sœurs knew—her neighbours, the drugstore clerks, her clinic's medical team, her women friends, and her brothers, too—but her own son was too busy, too important, she supposed, to take an interest in her lot.

Adam still stood in the doorway. He flashed his most winning smile, pointing out that he'd brought her maple syrup. Thérèse showed neither surprise nor joy. Which was par for the course.

A menthol cigarette smouldered in the ashtray on the coffee table next to a cup of tea; his mother had been sitting in the living room when he knocked. On TV was a lively talk show, the kind of catch-all program that discussed the virtues of kombucha and medical assistance in dying over the course of the same fifteen minutes. At the production team's Christmas party, the host of the show got into a tequila-shot challenge with a popular actor and, as he was leaving, Adam saw her throwing up into a snowbank, then conscientiously covering up the mess with fresh snow.

"Happy birthday, Maman." Adam held out to his mother the bottle of syrup, a pretty—and unlabelled—glass bottle with a tiny handle that contained five hundred millilitres of amber liquid, in other words, about one per cent of his harvest. Adam had tied a red bow round the neck.

"Sugar's a poison, you know," his mother said by way of thanks.

"You don't need much. It's very flavourful. Sylvain says— that's my...that's his family, the Sweet family—the land used to belong to them, and when I bought it, I asked them to stay and work on the maple stand with me. To train me. In any case, Sylvain says it's an exceptional year. Because of the huge shifts in temperature. Cold by night, hot by day."

"Yes, it was awful. I've slept poorly for months."

"You can turn up the heat at night if you're cold."

"It's central heating. I already told you that, but you've gone and forgotten."

Adam nodded. The choreography was one they'd perfected. Over time, he had gone from six annual visits to four, then down to two. This was the first time he'd seen her since December.

"Sorry, Maman."

"I don't know why you're apologizing. I'm just stating a fact."

"I can speak to the building manager if you'd like."

"I'm surprised you found time to drop by today."

"We're only celebrating Marion tonight."

"Hmmm. How old is she again?"

"Forty."

His mother let out a low whistle. A mocking one, it seemed to Adam.

"You and she have a thirty-six-year age difference, to the day. She sends her love, by the way."

Actually, Marion had not asked him to convey any message at all. She usually came with Adam and held his hand till he knocked on the door. She'd offer to make tea, go out to buy cookies or the oat biscuits Thérèse liked. She'd bring flowers.

"Thanks for reminding me just how old I am."

"Sorry, Maman."

His mother sighed. They were at the stage in the dance where she signalled through her silence that he had gone too far, that he had pushed her to the limit and what had she done to deserve such a distant son: What did I do to deserve to be this alone, didn't I sacrifice everything, and your sister who hates me so much she moved six hundred kilometres away? Would it kill your children to come see me from time to time? When I had gifts for them, they made the trip. Oh yes, that they did, for Grandma's cheque in a Christmas card they showed up, but the rest of the year, not a thing, I don't exist. I only existed for you and your sister; did I not earn the right to criticize you for that? If not, where is my reward?

Bitterness had penetrated the walls and seeped beneath the wooden floors and behind the pictures in frames on the shelves.

Adam looked up at the television airing a commercial for the next episode of his show. He was seen visiting a producer of organic asparagus on Île d'Orléans, a scene shot the previous summer, before the maple sugar stand, before the holidays. Before Celia Smith's shattered knee in the salt water off Martha's Vineyard. Adam observed himself onscreen. An open expression, a spear of asparagus between his teeth. Sunshine flooded the fields and the river. Barely a year separated him from that Adam, an intact Adam. A year, a century, an eternity. Joe Dassin's "L'Été indien" started playing in his head and he felt like laughing. Was this the man they all saw in him, his mother, his children, Marion? The Sweets? What a performance.

"I'm leaving now, Maman."

His mother had dozed off. This woman, so proud, with copper highlights in the hair she'd worn pulled back in a full chignon since the seventies. As a child, Adam had loved to contemplate her profile until, eventually, she'd turn to him and snap, "Stop staring at me like that, it's intrusive." That unsinkable woman now slept in her armchair in broad daylight. Adam stubbed the still-lit cigarette out in the ashtray and waited, his phone glued to his ear, ready to feign a conversation when she woke so they could both deny that she had fallen asleep while he sat there.

He couldn't wait to leave.

AS HE MERGED ONTO THE HIGHWAY, ADAM USED HIS hands-free system to call Sylvain. It was almost three o'clock and traffic was heavy for a Saturday. By the time he stopped off in Oka, then Hudson to pick up Marion and join their relatives and friends, it would already be five and he would barely have time to change.

A wave of nausea hit him and he coughed to get rid of it. The sound of the ringing of his phone filled the car. Ever since filming had wrapped and the sugaring off had ended, each day stretched out before him like pasta dough, pale and rolling back in on itself. He only rose from bed after Marion left for the clinic, drank his coffee glaring at the high-voltage wire that neither winter nor despair had rid him of—his file was *making its way* through the municipal office, he'd been promised—then he took his car and drove onto the ferry. At the shack, he tinkered, picked up branches, cleaned his equipment, checked how the tubes were holding up. After that, he felt so tired he lay down on the cot.

At day's end, he'd find Marion in the shower or the laundry room and suggest thawing something out for supper, to which she'd agree with a distracted air. A new store offering ready-to-eat fare had opened in the village and kept them stocked with curries, dals, and pulled pork of acceptable quality, which had become essential to their diet. Adèle now lived in Villeray in a freshly painted apartment whose rent Adam covered almost entirely so they no longer had to worry about his daughter's dietary restrictions. On the day of her move, although they hadn't shed a tear, no one felt relieved. Despite the relative calm of his days, Adam collapsed into bed round nine o'clock, an hour for which he waited impatiently.

Today, not only had he paid a visit to his mother, he had a meeting planned with Sylvain—Sylvain had requested it and Adam hoped to see a renewal of their relationship, which he'd been at a loss to mend ever since the episode round the gin-and-sap liqueurs—after which he had to face a birthday barbecue with some sixty guests.

Sylvain answered on the fourth ring, just before the voice message clicked on.

"Sorry, Sylvain, it took me longer than expected at my mother's. I'm on my way and I'll be there soon."

Sylvain cleared his throat. "Oh, hi, Adam."

Adam got the impression that Sylvain was surprised to hear his voice. "Did you forget about our get-together? You're the one who scheduled it."

"No, no. I didn't forget."

Adam waited for what was to follow, but nothing came. "Hello?"

"I'm here, boss."

"What's wrong?"

Adam's heart flip-flopped. He touched his chest.

"I just wanted to tell you I won't be here for the next sugaring off. I won't be here over the summer either. I've got someone in my life now. Dominic. He's in Rivière-du-Loup. I mean, he was transferred there, he works for the federal government, and they had an opening, it tempted him—he's always dreamed of going back to his region. His parents live there. It'll be good for his daughter. Megan. She's twelve. That girl has got energy to burn, I tell you. It's great watching 'em together. She's his niece, but he adopted her when his sister and brother-in-law died. The little one was only a year old. A plane crash, can you imagine? So I said to him, 'Dom, I know it's only been a few months for the two of us, and usually nobody gives everything up for a single father they've just met on a dating site. You might think I'm crazy or somethin', but I'd really like to follow you there; I've got no family left.' Sure, I've got sisters, but they've had it, too. After Papa's funeral, we said it was time for us to do whatever we wanted: my sister Nat'll probably take a sabbatical. She wants to work with kids down south, in Haiti. I wanted to offer him that, to make a life together. He said yes. Boy, was I surprised. Just shows you never know. So, that's that. I'm moving on Saint-Jean-Baptiste Day, Adam, as soon as the little one's finished school."

Adam noticed that Sylvain had used his name. The involuntary "boss" earlier in the conversation had slipped out. A relic.

"We're going to sell the house. It's the last thing tying us to Oka now."

"You can't do that."

"Actually, you'd be surprised how easy a decision it was. All four of us agreed."

"I can hire you on full-time next year, cover all your expenses, you could go see them often, but you'd have a stable income here."

"That's nice of you, but no thanks."

"What will you live on over there?"

"I'm resourceful."

"Sylvain, no."

"You'll manage, Adam. You did great with the harvest. No need for you to come this far. That's what I wanted to tell you."

"I'm coming, we can talk face to face."

"Honestly, I've already thought it out."

The sun shone brightly and the asphalt on the highway looked almost white. Adam had a terrible headache.

"Not me, Sylvain. I haven't thought it out."

"Bye, Adam."

An suv honked insistently at Adam, who was about to change lanes as though he were alone on the road. As she passed him, the driver hurled a flurry of insults that he didn't hear—their windows were shut, each of them in their own air-conditioned bubble. Adam's heart pounded frantically in his chest and he thought, *I'm going to die here*. He crossed the highway's three lanes, took the first exit, and pulled over at the entrance to an A&W. He felt like crying, like screaming. But there was no relief, however painful, in sight. He was a prisoner in a parking lot, his sweaty hands clutching the steering wheel, his heart ready to quit, he was being hollowed out by a buried wail that pulverized everything in its path, a bomb dropped on a city of stone.

# 19

MARION WAS WALKING PATRICK TO THE DOOR JUST AS Adam drove up the lane, and she felt a moment's panic hearing the tires rattle along the driveway of crushed stones.

How would she explain Patrick's presence in the vestibule of their home?

*Patrick brought me some sheet music,* she could say, but the choir had given its end-of-year concert weeks earlier, so what would she be doing with it in the middle of summer?

*I forgot something in the rehearsal hall:* that was a better explanation.

But how could she explain away the state of Patrick's face—red and swollen from crying—and his devastated expression? Marion had just told him unequivocally that she had no intention of ever seeing him again—she had tried gentle hints, but Patrick was bent on playing the transfixed lover, coming as far as her own home, their home, professing eternal love—no, not at all, no, it wasn't a game, no, she hadn't felt anything since that last time in December, yes, she was telling the truth, and no, she wouldn't change her mind.

Marion hadn't planned on spending her fortieth birthday saddled with a lovesick man. Perhaps she had wanted a husband, children, a happy life, or maybe that was other people's wish for her? She no longer knew—in any case, she saw herself as an honest person. A *good person*. That was the biggest surprise of all: she had never been so mean and, yes, so undeniably in control.

She refused to give up one or the other. Honest *and* good. To manage that, she would have to hurt some people; she understood that now.

Adam's car was parked in front of the house, ready to head out again—they were expected at five, she'd said as much to Patrick to encourage him to leave. Adam slammed the car door and, during the few seconds during which he hadn't yet seen her, she was struck by the defeat in his eyes, by how much his body had changed. Fatigue dragged him down—his hair, his hips, his knees—and despite it all, he walked with a determined stride and the obvious intent to take her to the party, to put up with the balloons and the toasts; he would put up with this day because he loved her. He might collapse afterward, but not before delivering her to her fortieth birthday celebration. That's what you do for the people you love.

Adam caught sight of Patrick through the glass door just before entering. Patrick had his back turned and hadn't had time to prepare for the encounter. Marion said nothing. No words came to her.

Surprised by the sound of the knob turning, Patrick spun round. The two men stared at one another for a second. Not with scorn. It wasn't that kind of scene. It was one sorrowful man facing another, one of whom showed his sorrow more than the other.

Either Patrick had been crying or he had a rash; in either case, it wasn't normal. Adam looked at Marion. Patrick said, "I'm sorry, I'm leaving. Enjoy your evening."

Then he walked out, closing the door softly behind him so as to disturb no one. Marion listened to his footsteps along the loose stones until he reached the street.

And because Adam kept staring at her without blinking, as though he'd been turned into a statue in their vestibule, and because she found herself on the verge of a silence from which she would likely never escape, and despite the worse-than-bad timing—some sixty people waiting for them by pastoral tables decorated with seasonal peonies—Marion felt the words rise.

"Adam, I have to talk to you."

THEY ARRIVED AT THE PARTY TWO HOURS LATE; THE FIRST course's bubbly and bite-size tacos had already been served. "We couldn't lose our people," said Gisèle, determined that the party wouldn't founder.

As things stood, their Christmas had already been spoiled, so there was no way she was going to let her daughter's birthday get away from her—after all, it was her anniversary, too; it was she who had given birth, she who had bled and wept it had hurt so much, but what a wonderful hurt, and did you know that in the Netherlands, the mother is the one people congratulate on the day of her child's birth?—just because Marion was going through a *mid-life crisis*.

"Listen, your mid-life crisis had better be over because we can't take much more, my girl," she warned, opening the car door the minute they pulled up and, peering into Marion's face, happy to see she looked normal.

Yet there had been tears and a breakdown of sorts, but there'd been time for them to dry and fade on the drive to the party.

What had she told him? *I've slept with other men this year, oh, and with a woman, too. It doesn't mean anything.* Or maybe it did.

Is that what Marion said? No, surely not, it was unimaginable. Strange how the most decisive moments become muddled immediately afterward, whereas the memory of the clothes your chemistry teacher wore in high school twenty-five years ago remains intact.

Maybe she'd said, *I think I wanted to run away and did the opposite of running away, do you know what I mean?*

Adam looked at her with eyes awash in tears and nodded. They had slid to the floor, that she did remember, one on either side of the vestibule, unable to go anywhere else, to occupy that space. They'd faced each other, their backs leaning against the wall. Marion in her party dress and barefoot. Adam, his clothes rumpled and drenched in perspiration, his running shoes spattered with mud.

At last, Adam opened his mouth. "I just about died. I can't get over it."

And Marion: "Neither can I."

Adam continued, "The worst part of it now is that we can't go back to before. First, because we wouldn't know how. And then, because we wouldn't want to. But I'd so want to. If you only knew. But I can't."

———

Marion nodded. That was it exactly.

She told him everything. Patrick, Vancouver, her headlong flight. Her neglected parents. The jogger, *Anne of Green Gables*, the bartender; John, the baritone. The hockey game. Jessie's hurt, which Marion had dismissed. Christian. Odette Cohen's apartment. The breakfast of bacon and eggs. Adam cried, copious, sobless tears, a silent faucet.

Marion closed her eyes and covered her face with her hands.

Adam resumed speaking. "I wanted them to be my family. When I'm with them, I become like them: solid, genuine, useful. I wanted it so badly I bought their maple farm, Marion. I worked the earth of their land. I tapped the sap, hoping against hope I'd find their essence and that it would be transmitted to me. And that way nothing would haunt me anymore, nothing would confirm my emptiness, my awful banality; the evidence of my failures would be washed away, would evaporate. Marion, all I wanted was them."

Now Marion, too, was crying. She rushed to his side. They lay down on the cold ceramic tile floor and stayed there, in an embrace of numb stillness, almost falling asleep until they could no longer ignore the burst of calls and texts demanding, with growing rage, *where are you, where are you both?*

Gisèle preceded Marion and Adam through the entrance to the white tent set up on the lawn of the two-hundred-year-old estate she'd booked last fall to be sure. It was a dream venue for a wedding, and her daughter's fortieth birthday would be the closest thing to a wedding in their family. "Myriam won't be the one to spoil us on that front, and after ten years together, if you and Adam haven't made the leap, I think our chances are nil, right, Raymond?"

Raymond shrugged. "What matters, Gigi, is that they're happy."

"Of course it is, but you can be happy and still get married."

Marion had heard the same refrain for far too long and had decided that, if all it took for her mother to quit harassing her was to organize a monster party, then she would let her mother organize a monster party.

It made her so happy.

Everything had been ready for ages, and today the only thing they had to do was show up for the others and pretend their world hadn't just collapsed. Going back to her role from childhood, whose many rigid costumes she had discarded, layer by layer by layer, just seemed too much right now. The unsettled, fragile state with Adam didn't help matters either. Could there be some way out? The méchoui was ready, Yara was here, as well as Jessie, Suzanne, and Claude, who had pooled their money to offer her a one-year flower subscription.

"You love wildflower bouquets so much," explained Suzanne, "you'll receive flowers every two weeks in good weather and bad."

Adèle and Félix had come together without their mother, although she had been invited. Nearby stood a stooped, smiling girl. Sarah suspected her daughter was in love with this Léa, a friend who'd become a roommate, and was hurt that Adèle had hidden it from her. That's what Sarah had told Marion over the phone, a rare moment of her sharing, in the middle of a conversation about moving a bookcase Adam had given his daughter. "Do you think they're an item?" Marion's eyes welled up; this was the very first time Sarah had asked her opinion, just as their co-parenting—if that's what the arrangement could be called—was coming to an end. How sad. What treasures had passed them by because of their refusal to form an alliance?

Félix hugged his father, ruffling his hair in passing. Adam played along, glad for the mutual affection. Two puppies, two brothers more than anything. Then Adam pulled his daughter to him in an awkward joining of two tense bodies. Instead of freeing herself and avoiding Adam's gaze the way she usually did, Adèle took her father's left hand and pinched the delicate skin between his thumb and index finger. She did so with such confidence that neither Marion nor Adam thought to question her. Adèle looked at her father: "This is an excellent pressure point to calm anxiety. Try it for ten, fifteen seconds and it'll help. And nobody will see you doing it."

Disconcerted, Adam eyes searched out Marion. Adèle still held his hand as though it were a bird she'd scooped up after a collision with a too-clean window. Adam took a breath and an infinitely slow smile appeared on his face. Marion hadn't seen that smile in a long time, and never for his daughter. The small miracle of knowing you've been seen by your loved one. It was both beautiful and indecent.

The aunts, uncles, cousins. Simon, Julie, Adam and Marion's many friends. Children everywhere. *That's what filled their life*, Marion thought. It was one means among others—having children—of cheating death. Marion no longer felt the same cold wind at the thought that she wasn't a mother now that she understood that.

Raymond was busy taking pictures, a tear in his eye, so proud of her and so in love with his Gigi. Myriam had flown in and watched her from a distance, standing at the back of the tent, an almost empty glass in her hand. Marion felt like running over to her, gluing her forehead to her sister's, and whispering, "C'mon, let's get out of here." As kids, they could be found buried under the coats in the bedroom, laughing and sweating, sheltered from the boredom of grown-up conversations.

The méchoui was delicious, cooked to perfection, as was the sauce made with Adam's syrup. Raymond had spent the day supervising the rotating spit despite the presence of the chef, a friend from DNA's early days, who was now at the head of his own restaurant in Saint-Henri. The wines, specially chosen, followed one another, as decided by Adam's favourite sommelier, a deadpan woman who only slept in the morning and who, at the age of fifty-two, could be mistaken for a student. Due as much to her refusal to conform as to the vintage coveralls she wore day in and day out.

Marion had been so impressed by all of these people. Struck dumb in their presence.

In their eyes, who was she, this dull-blond dentist from the suburbs, some *dame*? Did they make fun of her whenever she left the room? Adam likely forestalled that.

Today she watched them busy themselves, lean in, a hand on her shoulder, and ask, "Is everything all right, Marion? Is everything the way you want it?"

She had to admit there was nothing fake in their tone, no visible hypocrisy. No, they just wanted her to be happy. Why had she imagined anything but? She hadn't changed, after all.

She hadn't gone from *empty* to *full*.

She had always been here.

Later, the chairs and tables were pushed back and everyone danced in a circle to their favourite hits. From time to time, Félix played lewd hip-hop only the young people or the restaurant staff had heard before.

It was a beautiful night, barely cool. It felt good to be outside, where the fragrance of peonies washed over them in waves. One group grabbed bottles of wine and blankets, and Marion jogged along with them down a slate-tiled path to the lake the manor overlooked.

On an Adirondack chair, wrapped in the blanket her mother used to bundle her in as a child whenever she was ill, Marion looked for Adam in the dark.

A very pregnant Julie sat nearby and sang with Yara one of Céline Dion's huge hits from their teen years. By the shore, shadowy figures threw stones and the ripples they formed could be seen on the water's surface under the light of the almost-full moon. Marion recognized Adam in their midst, his white shirt, his sleeves rolled up to his elbows. How she had loved those forearms. How she had clung to them. His stone skipped six times and his joyful laugh echoed across the lake.

"Marion, I made it to six!"

And Marion said, "I saw, I saw."

# Celia

CELIA SAID SHE DIDN'T FEEL LIKE GOING TO THE BEACH.

She was still in bed when she shouted back to her mother, who was having her morning coffee in the kitchen. Celia pulled the sheet up to her chin despite July's damp heat. Summer visitors thought the wind always blew here, a marvellous breeze that brushed against their faces as they nursed their drinks before dinner on the porch of their house with a view, rented for a few days or purchased for several million dollars, and that to live here year-round was a true gift from the gods. They'd often say as much to Celia and to those who, like her, had been born on the island.

"How lucky you are!" they'd exclaim, loading the groceries they'd paid for without a care into the gleaming suvs they ferried over at great expense.

They didn't know how suffocating and cloying the summer nights could be in the old apartments found in Oak Bluffs or Vineyard Haven, whose fronts were peeling from the salty air and a lack of income.

To say nothing of winter nights. Celia and her brother pulled on two pairs of woollen socks, one on top of the other, the minute they got home from school to lock in the heat from the school bus. Any day at below-normal temperatures brought a damp chill to the house that penetrated floors and bones.

Of course, the island did have its moments of glory.

AN OCTOBER AFTERNOON IN THE EDGARTOWN MARINA, free of all tourists, under the generous sunshine of low season, when Celia could claim for her own the light and the murmuring waves.

Mornings of storms, with their dense colours and symphonic movement.

Early spring, its fresh scents.

And, it had to be said, some summer evenings, too, and the new faces they brought: students come to work on the island or bored over their holiday with their parents, and who invited them, her girlfriends and her, to build a fire on the beach together or wander through the Oak Bluffs arcades until late at night.

Those dark, blessed hours during which she felt so light, and, to those boys, seemed so free.

But she didn't want to think about those distant nights, those boys. She didn't feel like going to the beach, didn't feel like getting up, or explaining, or pretending.

She was still bleeding, for six days she'd been bleeding when, after hers, Kiera had only bled for two days.

She reached out and opened the drawer to her night table. Inside a notebook chock full of her compact, bold writing, furious texts she didn't dare call poems yet. Removing it from between two pages, Celia read again a sheet of paper folded in four. *After an abortion, you may bleed for several days. That is normal. If the bleeding persists for more than a week or grows heavier and/or is accompanied by a fever or pain, contact the clinic.* Six days wasn't quite a week. And she had no fever or pain. She wouldn't call today.

Tomorrow, maybe.

"You promised the boys you'd take them," her mother reminded her from the kitchen. "If you lie around in bed any longer, you'll take root there."

Celia pulled the sheet up over her head and listened to the sound of her breathing under the sky-blue fabric. She liked the way the light filtered onto her skin. She had a distinct memory of the way waves approach, soon to disappear on the sand, the multiple hues they take on, in accordance with the water's moods. Almost white, then taupe, then a damp, earthy brown, and, underwater, a dark grey. This morning, she felt like her skin held every single one of those colours. That she was an abandoned seaweed, swaying beneath the current forever, neither dead nor alive. She had a vison of the seawater rising, rising to the dunes, covering the wooden stairs, then flooding into the parking lot, sweeping into the cars, flowing toward the streets, infiltrating their house, and ferrying away their furniture, the pink lamp from the living room, the one with a paper shade, the potted crocus, the toaster.

A vision that kept invading her thoughts at the most inopportune times, and she could do nothing about it.

In her mother's shop, counting squares of taffy before putting them in their cardboard boxes.

In the hotel as she smiled and took breakfast orders in the dining room.

In the bus taking her from Edgartown to Oak Bluffs.

In the Boston clinic last week as she lay on the examining table, her knees lifted and a gentle nurse with a high-pitched voice saying, "Hold my hand, hon, and squeeze as hard as you want."

Celia had squeezed hard and the nurse must have thought she was afraid of having the abortion.

When actually she was afraid of being swallowed up by tons and tons of water, raging torrents everywhere, water monsters engulfing her, and, with her, all that she knew and loved.

Her mother knocked on her door, a light rap, then entered without waiting for Celia's okay.

"So we're playing dead this morning," she said with equal parts lassitude and empathy in her voice.

The weight of her mother sitting on the edge of the bed created a hollow in the mattress. Celia pulled the sheet from her face and said again that she was tired, that she was still bleeding, and that she didn't feel like going to the beach.

Rhonda frowned, creasing her handsome and extraordinarily youthful—and impeccably made-up—face. She laid a hand on her daughter's brow and the warmth of that contact did Celia so much good that tears formed in the corners of her eyes before trickling down to the pillow.

"Sweetheart," Rhonda said, "this too shall pass."

One of her mother's favourite expressions, and one Celia also used to drive away fear, grief, or anger—the emotions she felt both reading the news and having to listen to some dude in class complain about the supposed hegemony of intersectional feminism.

*This too shall pass. As will the reign of humans on earth.* Celia took a deep breath, then shook her head.

"I was depressed the first time, too."

"The first time?"

Rhonda shrugged, looking somewhat sombre. "Someday I'll tell you about the second time."

"Why not now?"

"Because now you wouldn't understand."

"How do you know?"

"Generally speaking, children have no desire to know their mother deprived them of a little sister or brother."

Celia studied her mother, her short cut, a change after years of using treatments to straighten her hair. Celia had never gotten into it because Rhonda had often warned her about the vicious cycle, and, in any case, the strong stench of the hair products made her feel sick.

"I'm not depressed, you know."

Or, at least, not because of that, thought Celia. It's the ocean, Mom. The ocean is coming for us, I've been telling you that forever. If I say it again now, you'll look at me with fear in your eyes or worse, pity, maybe even guilt. And it's not your fault or mine: it's a relief not to be pregnant anymore, I don't have a single regret, and you shouldn't have either for your not-one-but-two abortions; in fact, it could have been three or five, Mom. That wouldn't mean you're heartless, or that we were disposable, or the fruit of chance, I mean, of course we were the fruit of chance, just as this island is the fruit of all kinds of chance: billions of grains of sand coming together and hardening and emerging from the sea and trees growing and humans settling. Everything is chance except the end of the world: now that, that's us, it's because of us, do you understand?

Celia said nothing of all that. It didn't come to her in the form of words, anyway.

"Was it during the Grand Return of my blessed father?"

Rhonda gave a clipped laugh. This was how Celia and Jeffrey had baptized the strange period during which their parents had resumed their relationship. Three weeks of false joy during which they skirted round each other in the apartment, pretending to enjoy themselves, fearful of what any intimacy between the four of them might blow apart. It was like living with a fox. Celia watched him secretly, holding her breath. A tall man, his posture identical to Jeffrey's. Her father didn't ask them any questions, but if they questioned him, he'd talk fervently about his missions in the Mediterranean, hundreds of missions to rescue migrants, and about the difference he and his team were making. At those times, Jeffrey said nothing, just put the dishes away with more clatter. He'd quit collecting Julian's postcards a long time ago. Celia would have liked to ask him whether they, too, weren't *a population he could have helped*, but at that age, she had yet to master rhetorical questions. When he was offered a prestigious position—aside from the salary, he'd grumbled—in Washington, he'd left, saying over and over how wonderful it would be to see each other more often now that he'd be within driving distance and the whole family pretended to believe him. After he left, Rhonda opened the windows wide to air the place out.

"I'll tell you some other day. I've got to look after the shop."

"I have nothing to forgive you for, Mom."

Rhonda smiled and kissed her daughter on the forehead. "Okay, up and at 'em, time to get some clothes on. The boys are waiting."

Alone again, Celia saw that her mother had left a cup of coffee for her on the night table.

Rhonda had been seeing someone for a few months now and everyone in the family knew he was rich—he was an architect and lived in a house he himself had designed and had built among the exclusive hills of Chilmark—but no one commented on it openly. What was there to say? *Mom, watch out, your new boyfriend is filthy rich?* The cliché would have it that he should be the one to watch out for her. As a single mother heading up a small family business, she'd been struggling ever since a new owner bought the building her shop was in and drastically upped the rent, so she had every reason to want to hook up with him.

In Celia's view, Kurt was the suspicious one. Something in his eyes—his eyelids half-closed as though he was forever laughing at a joke that only he knew the punchline to—didn't sit well with her. She wouldn't have trusted him with a single secret, let alone her mother's heart. But Kurt had a summer parking pass to Lucy Vincent Beach and had lent it to Rhonda, saying, "I know how much your daughter likes going to that beach." Ever since she was little, it had been Celia's favourite spot, she picnicked on Lucy Vincent's wild dunes whenever she could, off-season, when the islands' inhabitants were able to go there without having to prove they lived in Chilmark and handing over dozens of dollars.

So Celia, even though she hated the idea of owing Kurt anything, put the pass on the dashboard of her mother's old

Pontiac and crammed inside her two nephews; the threadbare beach chairs; the plastic ball; a few toys; and a bag full of licorice, chips, taffies—always—and bottles of water. She did it to make Sean and Anthony happy, but mostly Rhonda, who'd take advantage of Jeffrey's brief visit to go over the shop's budget with him, find any superfluous expenses; it would be a long and arduous process, and Rhonda would feel better knowing that they at least were having a good time.

It was a perfect day. The sky was partly cloudy, just enough for intermittent shadows to throw a protective veil across faces pulled taut by the sun, and the sea breeze raised the pretty whitecapped waves that children so love while, on the beach, no wind could be felt.

Celia chose a spot away from the other sunbathers, higher up on the dune where she could position the chairs without having to keep moving them back as the tide came in.

The beach was neither deserted nor crowded, another privilege of places reserved for the residents of wealthy areas; it felt like discovering an almost-virgin site, an Eden, the end of the world.

It felt like you were a winner.

Celia put sunscreen on Anthony's and Sean's backs and shoulders, on their necks, their bellies, their calves. The tips of their noses. She didn't think about the child she could have rubbed sunscreen on in one year, three years, or six years' time. There had been no child, really, there had not. It's normal when there's a miscarriage for women to talk about losing a baby, but when you've had an abortion, you don't. In both cases, you lose either an embryo or a fetus, depending on when the pregnancy ends.

One day, Simone, Jeffrey's wife, told her about a miscarriage she'd had three years earlier, before Sean was born, explaining that it felt like a heavy period.

Celia had wanted to know if she'd seen the baby fall. She'd used those exact words. *Did you see the baby fall?*

Her sister-in-law said there had been no baby. Blood, a few clots. But nothing she hadn't already seen during her periods.

Celia shook her head. "But you said you lost a baby," she said, immediately cursing her tactlessness.

Simone answered, "Just shows you what a strange beast reality is."

She also confided that the pregnancy had been unexpected and that she hadn't planned to have another child at that time—she'd had Anthony when she was twenty-two and just out of university. However, after her miscarriage, she became determined to get pregnant again to *put things right*, she'd said. And Sean arrived.

Simone had had her miscarriage at six weeks. Celia's pregnancy also ended at six weeks. Now she marvelled at the fact that their bodies had gone through the same thing, and yet not the same thing at all.

Actually, *marvelled* might not be the right word.

Sean wanted to build a sandcastle and Celia helped him fill his pails with wet sand by hand—they'd forgotten the shovel in the car. The children didn't feel like walking back to the parking lot and Celia couldn't ask five-year-old Anthony to watch over his little brother, no matter how briefly, while she went for it on her own. They would use their hands, and that would work, too.

Anthony was busy making an angel in the sand, waving his arms to create the most impressive wings possible.

"It's a sand Batman," he corrected her, and Celia took a picture with her phone to show later to Jeffrey and to send to Simone, who'd stayed in Atlanta for her work.

When she told them Anthony's comment, they'd say, *What an artist*, with the exaggerated pride parents express for their progeny, at least until the piles of stereotypical drawings or the same joke told over and over force them to admit under their breath that, more than likely, they have begotten an ordinary child.

We are better off acknowledging our ordinary nature from the outset. By having no illusions, we take away the power others have to crush them.

Sean walked ahead of Celia, his little legs still clumsy going downhill to the shore. Celia caught up with him and took his hand. It was hot and sticky.

A few minutes earlier, a seagull had swooped low over the beach and landed on the head of a little girl barely bigger than Sean. Her mother, all flustered, had chased the bird away, shouting. Sean had stopped playing to watch the scene, stock-still. Only his little belly moved in and out to the rhythm of his breathing.

Then he turned his big hazel eyes to Celia and told her the bird had to be forgiven because it was just looking for a place to land and the little girl's pink hat looked like a flower.

He said nothing more for a while, then added, "We'll forgive her mommy, too, because she was scared. That's why she turned into an eagle."

He bobbed his three-year-old head, satisfied with his reading of the event.

Now he was kneeling in the water and filling his pail while Celia, her hand shading her eyes, looked out to sea. She waded slowly into the waves, enjoying the cool water on her thighs.

A few swimmers off in the distance looked like small dots floating on the waves, as light as paper boats. The horizon had misted over, a change Celia found soothing.

She only saw the surfer at the last second, perhaps because of the mist, perhaps because of her sadness.

A man, in his fifties or so—to Celia all men took on the same hue after the age of forty-five—quite heavy, his hair longish and streaked with grey, and the pallid skin of white people who don't spend much time outdoors, was bearing down on them.

He seemed unsteady on his surfboard and his expression was unmistakable: sheer panic. At any other time, Celia would have laughed at his face contorted in fear, his eyes wide, his mouth agape. She would have laughed because it would have done her good to see someone fall who never falls anywhere else. She was not proud of that fact, but it was the truth.

Except that this man was bearing down on her and on Sean, who, his fists full of wet sand, had run toward her through the water, humming a made-up song in which birds apologized and mothers cawed.

Celia thought: *This is how the end of the world comes about. On a surfboard, the fault borne on the shoulders of some stupid tourist.*

She scooped up Sean, who thought it a game and cried out, like when the train accelerates on the roller coaster, which attracted the attention of Anthony, lying in the sand, and roused him to run toward them, too.

The surfer was trying to change the direction his board was headed; inexperienced as he was, however, he aimed it straight at them instead.

With Sean still in her arms, Celia tried to back away, but her feet sank in deeper with every wave, and she was stuck.

"Anthony, stay put," she shouted to her nephew on the beach, and Sean started whimpering that she'd hurt his ears.

Celia managed to extract her right foot from the wet sand. It took so much effort that she lost her balance; as she fell, she threw Sean far from danger before the board hit her left knee and raked her thigh. The man fell on top of her, apologizing, apologizing profusely.

Celia resurfaced, spluttering. Sprawled on the beach, Sean kept rubbing his eyes and calling, "Mummy, sand, Mummy, sand." In his fright, he'd forgotten who he was with but not who, in his life, solved all his problems.

"You're bleeding, Celia, you're bleeding!" Anthony cried, breathless, his gaze panic-stricken, a finger pointing at his aunt's leg.

Celia felt an electric shock along her calf and thought she'd been stung by a jellyfish, then she looked down at her legs.

Blood ran along the skin inside her thigh.

*Oh,* she thought, *I'm going to have to call the clinic, this much blood is too much.*

Then she understood it wasn't coming from between her legs. Her thigh was lacerated with thin red stripes, as though someone had used a needle to draw quick lines. Her brain registered the information at an astonishingly slow rate: Why did she have marks on her legs? What was she doing, weirdly sitting on the sand, drenched? Who was the blond woman leaning over her, her large breasts spilling out of her bathing suit, saying again and again, "Are you okay? Are you okay?"

Then the woman ran over to the man still floundering in the water, speaking to him in another language.

Celia could tell she'd asked him the same thing. Probably because of the rhythm. Or the worried inflection in her voice.

That's when she saw her knee. Or rather, that's when she saw the man stare at her knee as he emerged from the water. His eyes terrified, disgusted. The blond woman saw it, too, and clamped her hand over her mouth to keep from screaming. Then the other swimmers gathered round them. Then Anthony and Sean.

"Your knee's on backwards," Anthony whispered, like some terrible confession.

That's when Celia looked. A wave coursed through her body and she knew that it wasn't the ocean come to swallow her, that it was worse, and that this wave would swallow her from the inside out.

Later at the hospital, she will be told that she lost consciousness at that point, from pain, most likely, but that she screamed when the paramedics put her on a stretcher. Over the weeks of infinite boredom that will constitute her convalescence, she will often think of that scream she has forgotten. She will wonder if it was heard beyond Lucy Vincent Beach, beyond the fishing boats at sea, as far as the wild forbidden shores of Nantucket, its echo rattling there the tea services belonging to ladies gathered on majestic verandas to reign over the world, sheltered from it all.

When that thought surfaces, she will smile. But then she will get angry that it took her being shell-shocked to give voice to her outrage at the order of things.

"YOU'VE GOT A DISLOCATED KNEE, SWEETHEART," RHONDA said as she pulled the curtains when Celia regained consciousness an hour later in a hospital bed. "Only one torn ligament, a miracle, apparently, under the circumstances. Kurt says they could all have been crushed by the impact. Does it hurt?"

Celia shook her head. She felt weighed down and indifferent, nailed to the bed by a magnet.

"Too stoned to hurt, Mom."

"Good old morphine." Rhonda laughed softly. "I wouldn't mind some myself."

Celia closed her eyes to smile—unable to do more than one thing at a time.

"They'll be able to operate in a fortnight, sweetheart."

"What about the boys?"

"They went for a grand ambulance ride and the nurses gave them chocolate bars to tide them over till we arrived. The best day of their lives."

Rhonda gave a pinched smile and her eyes were damp. Celia held her breath. She didn't want Rhonda to cry. She didn't want her sorrow: that sorrow would lead her mother to Kurt, who would offer to cover the medical bills, gaining sway over her mother with all the ministrations Rhonda so desperately needed. Celia couldn't blame her, didn't dare assume the weight of making her understand that by accepting Kurt's gifts, she was bartering away the only thing she truly owned: her integrity—the wealthy had money and the prospect of fleeing, but soon not even money would do much good, they would all be reduced to survival mode, and then how would they ever manage to get up again if they sold their soul?

Mom, she wanted to say, don't be sad for me, it's only a knee, unambiguous pain, nothing at all, listen to me, what's important is to never, not for another instant or second of our lives, allow others to crush us, even out of love, even shaped by good intentions, let's free ourselves, Mom, let's free ourselves from those who don't understand, we'll confront the wave together. You were afraid for me, but you're the one who's most at risk, it's you, Mom.

"As soon as we're home, I want you to rest."

"Mom, I've got insurance with the university. It'll be all right."

"Who said I was worried?"

"I'm serious."

"It won't be enough."

"I'll figure it out."

"Forget about work for at least six weeks, you heard what the doctors—"

"I don't want Kurt to pay."

"Celia, your premiums will go up."

"Too bad."

"He's happy to do it."

"Let him find something else to make him happy."

"You've got the right to think what you want of him. But not to act like a little brat."

"It's decided," Celia cut her short.

A vexed silence flooded the room.

"Jeffrey thinks that…"

"What?"

"I mean, it's an accident."

"Yes?"

"But…"

"What?"

"It would be a lot simpler if you let Kurt look after everything."

"What, Mom?"

"Jeffrey thinks we could claim damages from the Canadian."

Celia stared at the brace round her knee. She wasn't in pain, but that comfort was artificial, controlled by medicine.

Later, when the pain had set in for real, radiating relentlessly from her knee to her foot, from her knee to her pelvis, when Celia had failed half of her fall semester courses, unable to get around quickly enough between the buildings and lacking the energy to study into the wee hours of the morning, when she had had to borrow money twice from her mother—which, of course, meant borrowing money from that clown Kurt—she would wonder what might have happened if she had taken her brother's advice: a formal notice, a lawsuit, being questioned at length in a lawyer's office as beige and grey as her brace. A win. The relief of money. An enemy made up there, north of the border, furious at the little profiteer's change of heart, who would harbour feelings of rancour toward her. Or worse, condescension. *I cried with fury—to be remembered with pity*, she murmured to herself, remembering words she'd just read written by Virginia Woolf, and she'd tell herself, *No, no, I did the right thing, I did the right thing.*

*I hurt, everything I am hurts, but I did the right thing.*

Over the winter session, she'd take the courses again, the ones she'd failed, and pass.

One day, they'll make a movie about you, her girlfriends would joke, one *based on a true story*, where the quest wasn't for love but one single woman's determination to change the world and save the planet. Moses for tree huggers, minus the patriarchy.

Celia would wave them off with a laugh, then say, "You know very well it's too late; for starters, movies are passé. Plus, the end of the world is already here, you know."

And her friends, used to her ways, would boo. "Shut up, Cassandra!"

Deep down, Celia knew they agreed with her; none of them held out any hope. But that was no reason to deprive themselves of laughter.

"Would you sue the Canadian, Mom?"

Rhonda raised a hand to rub the nape of her neck, a gesture Celia knew so well. Her lassitude, her body afflicted by so many repetitive movements, liquid sugar on the marble slab that had to be scraped, lifted, stretched, stirred. Only to start all over again, until exhaustion ensued.

Rhonda's fate was inextricably linked to the shop's; her parents had devoted their lives to it, and by the end, Herb was so stooped and gnarled he looked like an elf, a gnome sculpted out of wood and moss. He had done his utmost to keep the business going, taking on other jobs whose money he re-injected into maintaining and improving the premises. Despite his tenacity, he hadn't managed to keep ownership over the building and in the eighties had sold it to his neighbour, a shy gallery owner, who was independently wealthy and had promised to never terminate his lease. Until his death, Rhonda's father kept on the wall of his back office a photograph showing him arm in arm with the gallery owner he called their guardian angel.

"Look after him," he'd told his daughter when he knew his days were numbered, "because he looked after us."

And Rhonda had done her best. But eventually the gallery owner died—it's often the case once a person nears a hundred—and his heir, a distant niece living in Arizona, hadn't thought twice before accepting a purchase offer from a group of real estate investors well-known on the island for their over-the-top renovations and accordingly high rents. There had been no last-minute reversal of fortunes, no justice served, no victory for the little shop owner over capitalism.

There was only what was to come, belt tightening and local solidarity, overtime and sacrifice. Rhonda didn't sleep much. But hadn't she always operated on a sleep deficit? She didn't like people who complained. After all, she was the first of her line determined not to see her children take over the business. Jeffrey had settled in Atlanta with Simone as soon as he'd finished college; Celia had an ebullient future ahead of her: writing, politics, no matter. Rhonda would prevent any and all—including her daughter herself—from clipping her wings. One day Rhonda said, "Your love for the world is the most beautiful thing your father passed on to you." And Celia was quick to reply, "Let him just try to own that! Let's be clear: my love for the world comes from you, Mom."

*Ten more years*, Rhonda kept saying, *enough to reach retirement age. Then we leave the key in the door.* At those times, Celia scanned her expression to detect any lie, any disappointment. She saw none, or else her mother was very clever.

In the hospital room, Rhonda sighed. "You know what your grandfather said. Conflict begets conflict."

Celia nodded. She hadn't even told Miles when she found out she was pregnant. What was the point? The result wouldn't have made her change her mind, and the whole affair would have no more consequences for him than if the pregnancy test had come up negative. No parallel universe here, one in which they would have married and had many children. She'd followed a guy she met on the beach and spent three banal and entertaining nights that would change her life because every day changes us and affects us and draws us nearer to the end, just as the words written on the pages of a book lead us to its conclusion.

No more meaning than that.

He might have proven to be generous and empathetic, of course. Insisted on accompanying her or paying for the procedure, for instance. But he could also have been a coward or aggressive or worse. Happy to hear she was pregnant. Some guys adore the idea of having *sowed their oats*, and measure their vigour based on their capacity to reproduce, whether or not they participate in the daily task of looking after their progeny. Then, she would have had to explain. The certainty. The rising water. Her refusal to let a moment's negligence dictate her future—when she knew that it would be up to her to assume the consequences. And that she had a choice.

She would have had to speak the words, educate this summer tourist raised in cotton batting, this enthusiastic but novice lover, ill-prepared to understand the shakiness and complexity of the world in which she lived. Face to face with him, she would have felt infinitely alone and that would have made her angry because it's always the same; women are made to sort out the mess left between their legs and, worse yet, to grow through selflessness and sacrifice, and the hoax had gone on long enough, and she might have raised her voice. He would have said something tempting and inaccurate like "Since it took two of us to make this baby," and she would have cried, "Oh, yeah, the same way *it took both my parents* to make my brother before my father found a more 'promising' project, and the same way, eight years later, *it took the two of them* to make another child, me, before he left for sea again, the perfect cliché of the activist seafarer, is that how you mean *it took two*, Miles? No, what it took two to do was fuck, to lie on the quilt you stole from the cedar chest in the huge house your parents rented for the summer; it is deep kisses and loud moans of pleasure because the sound of the waves masked any noise we might make; what it took two to do was to decide to meet at the same place the next, then the next day, then early in the morning just before you left, behind the fishmongers', where you lifted up my skirt and slid your hand into my panties, saying, 'So that's where you're hiding,' and I laughed and you must have thought it was out of modesty when it was out of embarrassment for you, such dirty-old-man words coming out of your young prince's mouth, and you added, 'Don't be sad, I'll be back,' and I wanted to say, 'Who said I was sad?' but that would have hurt you and I kept quiet, of course; you would never have wondered, you say whatever crosses your mind, you let it out wherever you want, you have the right to be carefree, why wouldn't I demand the same, too? Why wouldn't I demand the same?"

That would have led to conflict. And conflict, her grandfather always said, begets conflict.

Around four, the doctor on call gave her permission to go home. They would phone her sometime over the next two to three days to give her a date for her operation should she decide to go ahead with it. In the meantime, she had to keep her knee immobile in the brace, be sure not to exert pressure on her leg, and take painkillers as required.

Jeffrey went to rent a wheelchair and helped her into it. Sean and Anthony each held one of Rhonda's hands, their big eyes fascinated by the wheels of the strange carriage.

He said, "At your service, your majesty."

She wanted to say to him, at last her revenge for all the years she'd been his scapegoat, but nothing came out.

Later she'd think: *The most precious thing the accident stole from me is my gift for a quick comeback.*

The loss was only temporary, but that's the sort of thing you never know in advance.

They were crossing the emergency waiting room on their way to the exit when she saw them. Celia noticed the woman first. She jumped to her feet, her hands clutching her straw hat, an oversized, immaculately white contraption bordered with a line of black pompoms, halfway between a sombrero and a panama hat.

The woman seemed suddenly aware of how ridiculous her hat was and threw it onto a chair before advancing on them.

"We wanted to be sure you were all right. Adam's all right, I mean, he inhaled water and we've got to watch for signs of secondary drowning, I suppose you've been told the same, but more shaken than hurt, right? More shaken than hurt."

Her left eyelid began to twitch, as though the woman were slapping herself inside for her stupidity.

"We don't mean to bother you. We asked at the reception, but the nurses wouldn't give us an update on your condition," the woman resumed, then quickly added that she understood, it was only normal, they weren't family members.

The man held back, his eyes lowered. He seemed ready to burst into tears, and Celia stared at him, not purposefully trying to challenge him—but aware of the discomfort she was causing.

What have you got to cry about, you moron? she screamed inside. What have you got to moan about like some spoiled brat who's just dropped his ice cream on the sidewalk? Boo-hoo, you swallowed a mouthful of water. Poor baby. This too shall fucking pass, you hear me? You're feeling guilty? It's the least you can do. I can give you a thousand other things you can feel guilty about, give me five minutes and I'll grind you into powder, go on, just one tear trickling down your cheek and I'll blow it all sky-high.

Rhonda laid her hand on her daughter's shoulder and a current passed through Celia, cutting short any lecture, even unspoken.

Her hand said *don't go there*.

It wasn't because her mother feared a scene or didn't have the same impulse. Exasperation. The acute awareness of the unfair distribution of misfortune here below.

What her mother's hand on her shoulder told her was *save your strength, it's to be used for you, this fury, it's for you the engine, for you the gas. And can't you see how pitiful they are?*

Celia blinked and looked again at the woman, whose ashamed face glistened.

"We're so sorry about what happened."

"Thanks."

The glow of Rhonda's pride, an owl in the moonlight.

"If there's anything we can do…"

"It'll be fine."

"Do you…do you have insurance? I know how outrageously expensive health care is here."

"We've got everything we need."

Celia noticed her brother's clenched fist and her heart swelled with love for him, this broad-shouldered man who, as a boy, had worn rocket-patterned flannel pyjamas for years, until the pants hem reached his knees and his belly showed under the shrunken top. He loved sticking his finger into his belly button. Celia would shudder in disgust and slap him. Jeffrey would laugh and push her over so she too would laugh.

Now she felt like taking her brother into her arms and showering him with kisses, swearing allegiance to him forever, convincing him to accompany her back to that wonderful time when they'd been children. He would have said it wasn't a wonderful time at all.

"We'd like to give you our contact information, just in case."

"It'll be fine."

"Mom," Jeffrey tried.

"It'll be fine."

Neither Celia nor the man had spoken yet. She could feel how on edge her brother was and that, above all, the explosion mustn't come from him.

She cleared her throat and everyone looked at her. Even the man, now leaning against the back of a chair, as though afraid he might faint, raised his eyes to her.

They were grey, his irises shimmering in what looked like a blend of blue and green that had been thinned by a paintbrush to dissipate the concentration of hues. Keeping his eyelids open seemed to require significant effort on his part.

Celia wouldn't see him cry, she understood that now. Not because he wasn't tormented—that was absolutely clear—but because he couldn't manage it yet. The level of water had begun to rise, like the horizon as one draws closer, and Celia saw that, soon enough, his whole being would be submerged.

She saw the man drown: his mouth, his throat, his airways, his lungs full of water—from tears, yes, of course—and the undertow that would take his wife with him, small stones from the bottom of the sea strewn through her blond hair, her bruised swollen body amid the parasols and towels and bottles of sunscreen the water had also swallowed, her straw hat floating on the surface, the only proof to be found of their existence.

*We will all be swallowed up, won't we*, Celia thought slowly, and a wave of grief and pain almost made her cry out in the waiting room of Martha's Vineyard's hospital, surrounded by children with broken arms and tourists suffering from sunstroke; a wave of grief and, yes, despite herself, against her will, of love for this grey-eyed man going under. A tear, a single tear, sprang onto her right cheek and, trickling, followed a winding trajectory along her nose to the corner of her lips, speeding up along the curve of her chin before it fell onto her red shorts, leaving a dark trace, as though a drop of blood had landed there.

Then she saw the terror in the man's eyes. Perhaps he was afraid of her; that was a possibility, she had the ability to frighten others, at least that's what people had always told her, whereas she herself wanted only to shout back that she was the one who was terrified by what she saw.

But this time she understood: it was more than that—the man's terror came from what she had let him see, without saying a word, and what he'd sensed in her eyes. She had shown him the future and he wouldn't get over it.

It wasn't revenge. She had chosen nothing about this encounter, this accident that would forever be indissociable from her story. It was the handing over of something like a burden, he the one, among all others, with whom it was to be shared.

And suddenly, this love, this compassion. This she definitely had not chosen.

Celia took her mother's hand. "Shall we go?"

Rhonda, sombre and proud, nodded.

Jeffrey relaxed and began pushing the wheelchair toward the exit.

As they waited for the sliding doors to open, Celia cast one last glance at the man and the woman, separated from her by the glass cage of the vestibule. They looked almost blurred, deprived of their real contours, and the reflection from outside projected onto them the pattern of the tall trees outdoors buffeted by the wind as it picked up.

# ACKNOWLEDGEMENTS

THANK YOU TO GABRIELLE RIVARD HILLER FOR THE SHORT education in sugar-making and the delicious gin-and-sap liqueur.

Thank you to Chloé Savoie-Bernard for her keen and sensitive read.

Thank you to Isabelle and Benoit for that unforgettable trip to Martha's Vineyard in 2016.

Thank you to Geneviève, Jeanne, Kiev, Caroline, Marie—matchless liberators of wild horses.

Thank you to Sam, Darius, and Hippolyte for all of life: to my family for their support and trust; and to the valuable friendships I am so fortunate in having and to the meaning you give to writing.

FANNY BRITT is a playwright, writer, and translator. She is the winner of multiple Governor General's Literary Awards, a Libris Award, a Joe Shuster Award, and was nominated for a Governor General's Literary Award for Children's Literature. *Faire les sucres* won the Governor General's Literary Award for French-language Fiction in 2021. Britt has written a dozen plays and translated more than fifteen works by many American, Canadian, British, and Irish playwrights. Born in Northern Quebec, Britt lives in Montreal.

SUSAN OURIOU is an award-winning literary translator and fiction writer. She has been a finalist for the Governor General's Literary Award for Translation on seven occasions, winning for her translation of *Pieces of Me* by Charlotte Gingras. She also translated Catherine Leroux's *The Future*, winner of CBC Canada Reads in 2024. Ouriou is the author of the novels *Damselfish*, shortlisted for a Writers Guild of Alberta award, and the critically acclaimed *Nathan*. She is the editor of two anthologies, the trilingual *Beyond Words: Translating the World* and the bilingual *Languages of Our Land: Indigenous Poems and Stories from Quebec*. She lives in Calgary.

PHOTO: MARNIE JAZWICKI OF JAZHART STUDIOS

Colophon

Manufactured as the first English edition of
*Sugaring Off*
in the fall of 2024 by Book*hug Press

Copy-edited by Shannon Whibbs
Proofread by Stuart Ross
Type + design by Ingrid Paulson

Printed in Canada

bookhugpress.ca